Hell Squad: Cruz

Anna Hackett

Cruz

Published by Anna Hackett
Copyright 2015 by Anna Hackett
Cover by Melody Simmons of eBookindiecovers
Edits by Tanya Saari

ISBN (eBook): 978-0-9941948-4-8
ISBN (paperback): 978-0-9941948-8-6

What readers are saying about Anna's Science Fiction Romance

At Star's End - One of Library Journal's Best E-Original Romances for 2014

The Phoenix Adventures – SFR Galaxy Award winner for Most Fun New Series

The Anomaly Series – An Action Adventure Romance Bestseller

"Action, danger, aliens, romance – yup, it's another great book from Anna Hackett!" – Book Gannet Reviews, review of *Hell Squad: Marcus*

"Action, adventure, heartache and hot steamy love scenes." – Amazon reviewer, review of *Hell Squad: Cruz*

"Hell Squad is a terrific series. Each book is a sexy, fast-paced adventure guaranteed to please." – Amazon reviewer, review of *Hell Squad: Gabe*

Don't miss out! For updates about new releases, action romance info, free books, and other fun stuff, sign up for my VIP mailing list and get your free copy of the Phoenix Adventures novella, *On a Cyborg Planet.*

Visit here to get started:
www.annahackettbooks.com

Chapter One

Crouched in the shadows on the roof of a half-destroyed bank, Santha Kade looked through her high-tech binoculars and watched the alien invaders patrolling the streets below.

A year ago, these dinosaur-like raptors had decimated the Earth. Their huge ships had appeared in the skies...then they'd launched a vicious, unforgiving attack. Now they had bases in all of what was left of the planet's major cities.

Here in Sydney, the once-shining capital of the United Coalition, they'd ruthlessly razed the city. They'd left skyscrapers in tatters, the Harbor Bridge a shattered ruin...and humanity broken, afraid and on the run.

Santha's hands curled around her binocs. So many had died. Millions of lives...gone. Some survivors remained hidden in what had once been their homes, but they were slowly moving on or being weeded out by the raptor patrols.

She reached for her weapon. Her hand closed on her Titan tactical crossbow—the metal was cool under her fingers and the self-loading mechanism was filled with her own homemade bolts—and she felt herself grow calm, steady. Some gave up, some ran…and others chose to fight back.

She zoomed in with the binocs and studied the face of the lead raptor. Thick, gray, scaly skin covered his elongated face and his eyes were blood red. The aliens were all big—over six and a half feet—and carried a lot of muscle. They wore a kind of metallic armor on the bottom half of their bodies, and huge boots. Their top half was all tough skin, crisscrossed with what looked like leather for holding their claw-like blades, or for the snipers, their bone-like projectiles.

Looking at them made Santha's throat close in a choking rush. Why the hell had they come here? Why, with no warning, had they decimated the human race? Destroyed friends and families. Killed beloved sisters. She lowered the binocs and gripped her thigh. Her fingers dug into her skin through her black cargo pants.

It didn't matter. She didn't care. Whatever their reasons, she was going to make them pay.

Focused, she lifted the binoculars again.

The raptor at the back of the patrol came into view and a muscle ticked in Santha's jaw.

This one was the leader for this area. Santha was sure of it. She'd been spying on them for months, taking notes, marking down their installations, picking off small raptor patrols when she could.

She wouldn't ever be able to find the raptor that had beaten her sister to death, but she could sure as hell take down the one who'd given the order.

Who'd brought these aliens here and ordered them to kill.

This raptor was a little taller than the rest, skin smoother and a darker shade of gray. Santha had nicknamed this alien, *the commander*. The commander had an air of authority and looked at everything like it was his—or her, who knew what gender they actually were?—domain to rule.

Not for long, asshole. Santha lowered her binoculars and took a deep breath. She wanted to leap off the building and shoot the commander through the goddamned head. Another deep breath. But not today. She needed more intel first, and she wanted to take out the leader and their main base in the city.

She caught a movement in the sky out of the corner of her eye. As she stared at the bright, blue expanse, she didn't see anything but fluffy white clouds.

She kept staring. *There*. A blur of something winked for a second.

Santha knew what it was. A Hawk quadcopter, with its illusion system up, flying in from the west.

Other humans were fighting back, too. From a secret base west of the city.

She watched where she guessed the camouflaged Hawk was flying and wondered if Hell Squad was on there. If *he* was on there.

She only had a little contact with the few survivors still hiding in the city. Most had left for the country or for Blue Mountain Base—the underground military base that had become a haven for survivors. But everyone had heard of Hell Squad. A group of soldiers so deadly, they mowed through the aliens as easily as taking an afternoon stroll.

Normally, she would have written that sort of reputation off as exaggeration, but she'd seen them in action. She'd even helped them a couple of times.

And she watched them…a lot.

Especially the sexy soldier with the dark, liquid eyes, sensual grin, and an accent that made her insides flutter.

Cruz. His name was Cruz Ramos.

She'd met him several weeks ago, when she'd helped them fight off aliens so the squad could get in to destroy a key raptor communications hub. Hell Squad had blown the damn thing sky high. And for a month, the raptors had scrambled around with limited communications. It had made Santha's job a hell of a lot easier. She'd spent days out picking off lone raptor patrols who couldn't call for backup, and blowing up their facilities.

But they'd recently repaired the damage.

Santha shivered and shifted her binocs to where she'd last seen the Hawk's illusion. She caught a glimpse of gray steel as the copter dropped lower to land. She told herself to stop watching and focus on the raptors instead. After a quick—and futile—mental debate, she lifted her binocs again.

Zooming in gave her a perfect view of the now-visible Hawk in an empty parking lot. The side door slid open and a big man with broad shoulders and a scarred face leaped out, laser carbine clutched in his hands.

Marcus Steele. Hell Squad's leader.

Another man followed, with an intense face and a shaved head. He was a mix of races, but from the shade of his dark skin, she'd guess one of his parents was black. The predatory way he moved told her he knew how to fight, and that you didn't want to meet him on the battlefield and be on opposing teams.

Two more people exited the Hawk. A man and a woman. Sniper, by the looks of the lanky man's long-range rifle, and a dark-haired woman who looked like she ate nails for breakfast, lunch and dinner.

Then a young man leaped out. The sun glinted off his blond hair and eager face. She knew Hell Squad had lost one of their team to the raptors about a month back. She guessed this green kid was their replacement.

Then her heart leaped. *Cruz.*

He landed beside Marcus and was saying something, even as his gaze scanned the area around them.

Okay, so the way the man was put together worked for her. No harm in looking. He was shorter and leaner than his teammates, although by no means soft. She wished she could see through his black body armor. Santha bet the view beneath would be just as fine as his handsome face. And oh boy, that was a hell of a face.

Then Santha thought of Kareena. Her sister had been so beautiful and full of life. And now she was no longer here to tease Santha about her interest in handsome men.

Santha moved the binoculars away from Hell Squad.

She was out here to get revenge for Kareena. Not ogle Cruz Ramos.

Then Santha caught movement about a kilometer from Hell Squad's landing spot. *Raptors.* Crouched amongst the ruins of a small office building.

She zoomed back to the Hell Squad. They were moving now, led by the sniper and the tough-looking woman. The team moved together like a well-oiled machine, something she knew took practice. She'd been like that with her team. A pang hit her as she thought of the men and women who'd been like family to her. Now all dead.

Then she noted where Hell Squad were headed. Toward the raptors.

She swung back to the aliens, and spied the small dish set up near the top of their hiding place. She knew what it was. A jammer. It would jam the feed from the drones Hell Squad used to locate the enemy.

Hell Squad were moving right into a raptor ambush.

Dammit. Her heart kicked against her ribs.

Standing, she slung her crossbow over her shoulder, then grabbed the line she had tied to the top of the building. With her Kevlar gloves on, she simply gripped the rope and swung off the side of the building in a wide arc, sliding down to the ground.

Her feet hit concrete and she bent to absorb the impact.

A half-second later, she was sprinting for her bike.

***

Cruz Ramos kicked his boot through some rubble on the street. Under the pile was a small, tattered teddy bear.

He crouched and picked up the toy. He wondered what had happened to the child who'd owned it. Cruz looked up and scanned the empty houses. Some splintered doors stood open, the roofs damaged, windows broken, the walls smoke stained. Other homes looked perfectly normal, like a happy family still lived inside.

He wanted to believe the child had gotten away, maybe made it to Blue Mountain Base. But inside, Cruz felt a growing numbness. He dropped the toy. He knew what had happened to the kid who'd loved the stupid bear.

Sometimes he wondered why the hell he and the squad bothered. Fighting off the empty, dark feeling, he focused on the rest of his team.

Marcus was nearby, alert for anything that might crop up, and murmuring to the team's communications officer through his comms device. He was a hell of a team leader, always had a plan B when shit hit...which it always did. Hell Squad got the best missions.

In his own earpiece, Cruz heard their comms officer, Elle, laugh at something Marcus said. Cruz almost smiled. She did a hell of a job providing their intel...and she was also officially the love of Marcus' life. Cruz shook his head. He'd watched the two of them dance around their feelings for months. He would never have guessed slim, classy Elle—former society girl—and rough, tough, battle-hardened Marcus Steele would be a match made in heaven. But they fit.

The team's sniper walked past Cruz, followed by Hell Squad's female team member. For once, Claudia and Shaw weren't bickering. A minor miracle. They were both quiet and focused.

"So, we gonna whip some raptor butt?"

The voice from beside him made Cruz roll his eyes. "Kid, you want to keep your voice down."

A clearing throat. "Right."

Sam Jenkins was on a trial run to fill the empty slot on Hell Squad. The best soldiers were already on the squads, so the pickings were slim for replacements. As far as Cruz could tell, Sam was young, eager, but with limited experience. He'd been in the United Coalition Military Academy when the invasion had hit. His shininess would either wear off real quick and he'd quit, or he'd get himself killed.

Cruz glanced at Gabe, who was just a little behind them. He had a way of moving that was spooky and completely silent. He could disappear into shadows in the blink of an eye. His brother had been almost as good.

Jesus, Zeke. Whenever Cruz thought of their fallen teammate, he felt a flood of anger. But even that flash of emotion faded quickly. Consumed by the growing deadness inside that he couldn't seem to shake.

Death. Destruction. Blood and fighting.

Sometimes, he couldn't remember what he was fighting for anymore.

Something tingled along Cruz's senses. He slowed, turning his head to study the surrounding buildings. Nothing moved. Even the air was still.

He stopped and turned in a slow circle.

Marcus held up a closed fist. The team halted.

"Cruz?" Marcus murmured.

Cruz couldn't see or hear anything that should have set off his internal alarm. "I don't know, *amigo.*" But something was wrong.

"Marcus?" Elle's voice. "We've lost the drone feed. I can't see you guys or what's around you."

As Marcus cursed, Cruz's gut cramped. Yeah, something was really off.

Then he heard a noise. Cruz spun, and straight ahead, speeding toward them, was a slim figure in black. Her black hair flew out behind her and he saw the tip of her crossbow over her shoulder.

Santha. Everything in him flared to life.

Her sleek, black bike was electric and made no sound. Perfect for sneaking around the city.

As she got closer, he saw her face, watched her wave one arm at them madly.

Shit. "Everyone, take cover!" he yelled.

Seconds later, raptors streamed out of a building

ahead. Their weapons made a distinctive noise as they fired. Dark-green ooze splattered the road in front of the team. It sizzled and hissed as it ate through the asphalt.

He knew the damned stuff burned and paralyzed. He ducked in behind an abandoned car. *Madre de dios*, another thirty seconds and they would have walked right into the raptor cluster fuck.

Looked like the aliens had fully recovered their communications and were out for some payback.

Hell Squad dived for cover. Cruz watched Santha coax more speed from her bike. Even with the gunfire, she rode straight, heading for him.

She skidded the bike in a tight turn and came to a stop beside him. "Ambush. Had to warn you."

With a nod, he sprung to his feet and leaped on the back of bike.

She swiveled. "What the hell are—?"

"Ride."

She did. They raced through the raptors. Cruz aimed his carbine and pulled out his secondary weapon, a smaller laser pistol. He fired both weapons, taking down any raptor in range.

Santha turned the bike again and Cruz held on his with knees. They moved through the aliens again and Cruz kept firing. His team members were firing as well.

He and Santha did another loop. She anticipated his needs, slowing down, speeding up, tuning to avoid the raptor gunfire. Even in the middle of hell, he took a second to appreciate her lean body pressed back against him.

Then he saw a huge raptor, over seven feet tall, dragging Sam across the ground by his ankle. The young soldier was struggling and had lost his weapon.

Dammit. "Slow down!"

She did and Cruz leaped off the bike.

He unloaded his carbine into the raptor. It took a rain of laser fire, but the giant raptor finally tumbled to the ground like a felled tree.

Sam lay writhing, his right leg bent at an odd angle. Cruz yanked the kid up and hefted Sam over his shoulder. The kid probably weighed more than Cruz, but the slim-line exoskeleton in Cruz's armor helped him lift heavy loads. He ran for cover.

Behind an overturned minivan, he set Sam down. The kid was moaning, his eyes wide and jittery. "T-thanks, Cruz."

Claudia appeared. "He okay?"

"Leg's broken."

"I'll take a look."

The team didn't have a field medic, but they all had basic training. As Claudia splinted Sam's leg, Cruz ducked out of cover to check on Santha.

She was still on the bike, riding toward the remaining raptors. She held something in her hand.

He frowned, and then, when he realized what it was, he grinned. Damn, she was his kind of woman, a queen among warriors.

She tossed the grenade into a group of raptors then made a tight turn on the bike. She rode back, standing up to make a small jump over some rubble. Behind her, the grenade exploded, flames reaching into the sky. The screams and grunts of wounded and dying raptors filled the air.

"They're retreating." Marcus' gravelly voice came through Cruz's earpiece.

The last of the raptors slipped away through the ruins in full retreat. Warily, gun up, Cruz walked into the middle of the street.

Santha stopped her bike with a skid. The rest of Hell Squad came out of cover.

"Thanks for the warning and the help," Marcus said.

She nodded. "You should get going. Their usual MO is to come in with a larger force, and a pack of canids."

Cruz grimaced. He hated canids. The alien hunting dogs were vicious and relentless.

Marcus cursed. "We were supposed to check for some survivors our drones spotted in a school about a block from here."

Santha shook her head. "They left three days ago. Don't know where they are now."

Marcus nodded. "Thanks." He touched his ear. "Elle, can you send a Hawk our way and have the doc meet us back at base? Jenkins is injured." Marcus glanced at his team. "Hell Squad, let's move out. Gabe, carry Sam."

The armor's exoskeleton meant that carrying a team member, even for several hours, wasn't hard, but Cruz knew Gabe probably didn't need the help of the exoskeleton.

Cruz stepped close to Santha. "Come with us."

Another shake of her head.

He moved closer until his body was just a whisper from hers. He smelled her—sweat and a fragrant woody scent. "Come back to base. There's a place for you there."

"I'm not leaving."

Dammit. Cruz barely resisted the urge to kick something. He hated the idea of her out here, alone. "Why not?"

Her green eyes flashed. "I have work to do."

He leaned closer and saw her stiffen. "Don't you get lonely?" he asked quietly.

"You think being with a bunch of strangers will help with that?" She tilted her head. "You're with people all the time and you're still lonely."

Cruz felt his muscles tense. He stepped back. "What are you going to do?"

She revved the bike. "Keep fighting."

With frustration like a noose around his neck, he forced himself to nod. "Don't get yourself killed."

She flashed him a smile. The first he'd ever seen from her. "Sure thing, soldier."

She gunned the bike and shot away.

Cruz watched her disappear from sight. Yeah, she was right. Even surrounded by his team, he was lonely as hell.

Chapter Two

Cruz gripped the side of the Hawk as the four rotors swiveled and it began its descent.

They lowered through a circular opening, covered by retracting doors that blended into the surrounding forest. General Holmes, the head honcho, worked damn hard to keep the base a secret from the raptors.

As soon as the Hawk's rotors stopped spinning, Cruz leaped off. He was tired and smelled like sweat and raptor blood. He scowled. He'd have to make do with a cold shower, though, since hot water was only available in the morning. The geek squad were working on squeezing more power out of the high-tech solar power system, but when it came to powering the base, hot water was the lowest priority.

A few military personnel were bustling around the landing pads—mostly maintenance teams, logistics staff and pilots. Everyone wore a mix of uniforms blended with civilian clothes. Most arms of the United Coalition military had been decimated in the alien invasion. Whatever soldiers had survived had been cobbled together into the squads.

Even Hell Squad was a motley mix. They had UC Marines, like himself and Marcus, and the others were a mix of UC Army, Navy and SAS. But what they'd been before didn't really matter anymore. Now they were just Hell Squad, being sent to do the dirtiest, bloodiest fighting, again and again.

Once more, that nagging, empty feeling hit him. He unfastened his chest armor, pulled it off and slung it over his shoulder. The world was fucked. Nothing would ever be the same. It felt like they weren't doing much more than nipping at the raptors' heels, but even if they did fight them off—and that was a big if in his opinion—there would be so much rebuilding to do. Too much.

A headache started behind his left eye.

"Who's hurt this time?" Dr. Emerson Green bustled forward, her lab coat streaming behind her and her blonde hair swinging in a blunt cut that hit her jawline. Two medics waited with an iono-stretcher floating off the ground behind her.

"New recruit," Cruz said. "Sam."

"I take it he didn't make the cut." She waved at her medics to get Sam on the stretcher. Her gaze scanned the Hawk, running over each member of the team. Cruz saw the way her gaze stopped on the still and silent Gabe.

Yeah, they were all worried about Gabe. Since his twin brother had died, the usually quiet, intense man had become even more withdrawn. What Cruz didn't like most was the habit Gabe had of disappearing for periods of time with no explanation. He was worried Gabe was a ticking bomb...and Cruz didn't want Gabe, or anyone else, hurt if he happened to go off.

A slim figure came out of one of the tunnel entrances leading off the landing pads. She was running, her dark-brown hair flowing behind her. Her gaze zeroed in on Marcus and a smile lit up her pretty face. She launched herself at their team leader.

He caught her with one arm, yanked her up to his chest and slammed his mouth down on hers.

Elle Milton certainly wasn't the same person she'd been before the attack. A former society party girl, she was now Hell Squad's comms officer and she was damn good at it. She was also crazy in love with big, tough, scarred Marcus.

Watching them made Cruz's melancholy deepen. He was damned happy for his friend. If anyone deserved someone who looked at him like Elle did, it was Marcus. But watching the obvious connection between the two cut through Cruz like a combat knife. He pinched the bridge of his nose. Damn, he needed a good night's sleep.

Claudia nudged him with her shoulder. "Gabe and I are heading to the rec room for a beer." She shot a sharp look at the team's sniper. "And Shaw invited himself along to be annoying. Wanna join us?"

Cruz shook his head. "Rain check?"

"Roger that." Claudia sauntered away and shot a glance back over her shoulder. "Hey, your badass girl saved our butts again. We owe her."

His badass girl. Cruz fought a scowl. "Yeah."

He took the tunnel to his quarters. He was nearly there when Lainey, one of the base's schoolteachers, popped up beside him. He'd flirted with her a few times at the regular Friday-night parties. She was short, with dangerous curves and an open face. Pretty, fresh, and not afraid to show her interest.

"Hey, Cruz."

"Lainey."

She smiled, fiddling with her strawberry-blonde hair. "Would you like join me for dinner? A few of the other teachers are meeting in the dining room."

Cruz waited for the hit of heat. The stir of his cock.

Nothing. "Just got in from a mission. Not up for it tonight."

She leaned into him, her breast rubbing against his arm. "We could have a private party, then."

He should be all over it. Pounding his frustration out between Lainey's creamy thighs would be better than brooding. And it would feel a hell of a lot better, too.

But a long, slim body was the one that popped into his head. Dominated his thoughts. He didn't want the lovely Lainey.

He wanted Santha Kade.

"Sorry, Lainey."

The woman's mouth tipped downward, and she shrugged. "Okay. Catch you later, Cruz."

Since the invasion, in this small enclave of humanity, attitudes to sex had changed

17

dramatically. It was seen as a way to reaffirm life, to feel a connection when so many had lost their loved ones. And he'd been more than happy to partake at first.

But as he'd started to feel more disconnected, he'd begun to push the offers away. The last few months, drumming up interest in a woman had become too much work.

Until Santha had slammed a crossbow bolt into a canid intent on tearing him apart.

She'd saved Hell Squad more than once. She was out there, fighting the aliens. Alone.

Cruz slammed into his quarters, yanked off the rest of his armor and clothes and hit the shower. After the very cold water had washed away the filth, he nabbed a bottle of homebrewed beer from his mini-fridge and sat in the dark, nursing the bottle. He knew he should get out and shake off this dark mood, but right now, he didn't have it in him.

A knock at the door made him scowl.

He opened it to see Marcus standing in his doorway.

Cruz raised a brow. "You managed to drag yourself away from Elle?"

Marcus grunted and came inside. "Got a summons from Holmes."

A smile broke on Cruz's lips. General Holmes— in his early forties, highly educated with a distinguished air and a love of following the rules— clashed badly with Marcus's rough, tough way of doing things.

Cruz held up his bottle. "Beer?"

Marcus grunted his agreement and Cruz popped the top off another homebrew and handed it over.

Marcus sank into an armchair and took a sip. "Holmes got some intel that a group of human survivors are being kept prisoner by the raptors."

Cruz leaned against the small bench that made up his tiny kitchenette. "Prisoners? We've seen raptors take prisoners, but they're usually dead within a few hours."

"These ones have been there for months."

Cruz straightened. "Why? What are they doing with them?"

"Don't know. Learning our language, our way of life? Who knows with these alien bastards? A survivor made it here to base and said he saw these prisoners before he managed to escape. Said a Dr. Randall Lonsdale and a Dr. Natalya Vasin are among the prisoners. Two *genius* energy scientists."

Shit. "Who the raptors could learn a lot from."

"Yeah. And whose expertise could be used around here."

"When do we go in?"

Marcus took another long drag of his beer. "That's the problem. We don't know *where* they're being held."

"Shit."

"I suggested to Holmes that Santha could help."

Cruz straightened. "What?"

"She's been doing recon in the city since the raptors arrived. I'm guessing she knows their movements and where they're holed up better than anybody."

"Our drone footage—"

"Isn't enough. The raptors are good at jamming signals and are learning to dodge them. We don't have nearly enough info to find these prisoners. Santha might have seen something or knows something that could help us locate them."

Yeah, Cruz knew she'd be a big asset. That's why he tried so hard to convince to come with them. He gave a mental snort. Okay, that wasn't the real reason. She'd be a hell of a lot safer here at the base and she'd be here, near him. Just the thought of her was like a shot of adrenaline to the veins. "So we head in and find her."

Except they didn't know where she holed up. She always found them.

"Elle's started working on that. She's been marking the times we've run into Santha and locations where we know she's attacked the raptors. We should be able to narrow down a location and find her."

Cruz nodded. "Let's get to work."

***

The sun was setting, spreading shadows through the ruins of Sydney. Santha moved quickly and quietly. She only had twenty minutes to set the explosives before the raptors arrived.

She moved through the old gas station. The windows of the store were shattered, the shelves empty and a drinks fridge knocked on its side. Outside, the sign indicating the prices for gas, hydrogen and battery recharge had toppled, and leaves were piled up against the front door, rotting.

She'd seen the raptors using this place for storage. Putting something liquid in the underground storage tanks. She guessed it was some sort of fuel. She'd stolen a raptor ground transport once—an ugly, brute-looking vehicle that reminded her of a triceratops. It had run on some black, sludge-like substance.

Moving fast, she swung her backpack off and plucked out the small circular Nova charges, each about the size of her palm. They were small, compact and powerful. She pressed one to the side of the pump. A light blinked on—activated—then blinked off.

After the first wave of the invasion, Santha hadn't hysterically run through the streets, or headed west looking for the military to protect her. She'd broken into abandoned stores, and military and police installations, and stockpiled weapons, armor and explosives.

She glanced toward the west and wondered, just for a second, what it would be like to be safe and warm in Blue Mountain Base. And at the same time, she wondered what Cruz's warm naked body would feel like pressed against hers.

Sighing, she leaned her forehead against the cool metal of the pump beside her. He was destroying her concentration. She'd prided herself on her laser-sharp focus when she'd been on the

SWAT team. The guys had joked that nothing could distract Santha from her work.

Now her work was destroying the raptors. It had been the reason she'd kept living, kept breathing, for the year since the invasion. It had kept her warm at night, kept her company when the shadows of loneliness dogged her. She needed her focus now, more than ever.

With a shake of her head, she stuck another charge on the next pump and waited for the light. Revenge was all she needed. Warm bases and warm bodies were a luxury she couldn't afford.

She eyed the charges. One more should be enough. She didn't want to overdo it when she had no idea if what they were storing was explosive or flammable. She didn't want to leave a crater or set what was left of the city up in flames.

A growling sound echoed down the empty street.

The hairs on the back of her neck rose. With hurried movements, she stuck the last charge on the lid covering the underground tank. Then she shoved the rest of her stuff in the backpack and swung it onto her back. *Time to go.*

The snarls and growls got louder, followed by an almost wolf-like howl.

Except she knew these were no wolves.

They came into view, racing along the street in a vicious pack. Canids.

The canine-like aliens had thick, tough skin, spikes along their backs, and jaws filled with wicked teeth. They'd also developed a taste for human flesh.

Dammit. Santha sprinted back around the gas station building, squeezed through a hole in the fence and ran in the opposite direction. She lifted her gaze to the rooftops. Up was best. Canids could jump but they weren't the best climbers.

She spied an apartment building ahead. She'd scale the wall, wait the canids out, and then as a bonus, she might get to watch the raptors blow themselves to tiny alien pieces while she was at it.

But she was halfway to the building when raptor fire hit the ground around her. The green poison sizzled and hissed. She dived over it, rolled and got straight back to her feet.

Santha cursed under her breath. A raptor patrol was coming from the opposite direction, leaving her trapped in between. Eight of them, all armed.

She pulled her two Shockwave laser pistols from their holsters on her hips and fired. She didn't bother aiming. She just wanted enough distraction to get to cover.

Some of the raptors scattered, others kept firing.

Santha walked backwards, her green lasers lighting up the street. As she neared a shop front, she turned and ran.

The door to the grocery store stood open like a gaping mouth. She'd just reached it when raptor fire tore across her left thigh.

"Ahh." She almost went down but grabbed the door frame. The burning pain was indescribable. Panting, she pulled herself inside.

Fuck. The acidic poison was chewing through her trousers and eating through her skin. Now she was bleeding profusely, too, her trousers wet with her blood. *Not good.*

Gritting her teeth and fighting to stay conscious, she grabbed a grenade from her belt, ripped out the pin and tossed it outside.

She didn't wait to see what happened. She heard the bang, and the yells of the raptors, but she also heard the growls of the canids getting closer. She quickly grabbed a tube of med-gel off her belt, ripped the lid off with her teeth and squeezed the entire tube onto her wound.

Instantly, the pain eased a little. It was all she could do for the moment. She needed to get out of there...because the raptor poison also paralyzed.

Santha hobbled to the back of the store and out into a narrow alley. She hadn't gone far when she realized she was leaving a hell of a blood trail.

Shit. She squeezed her eyes shut. The pain might have lessened but it was still bad enough to have bile rising in her throat. She swallowed repeatedly and kept moving, but it wasn't long before she was dragging her leg and sobbing from the pain. The paralyzing effect of the raptor toxin was shutting down the muscles in her leg.

The canid yips and howls were getting louder.

She wouldn't make it. Not like this.

Santha slumped against the side of a building. After fumbling in the pouch attached to her belt, she yanked out a pressure injector filled with a blue liquid. She dragged in a breath, jabbed it into her good thigh and depressed it.

Wincing, she waited until the bracer shot hit

her. It was a cocktail of stimulants and painkillers designed for use by Special Forces troops on the front line. The advantage was it would hold off the paralysis and she could get away. The downside was that when it wore off, she'd collapse, out cold.

The bracer hit in a few seconds and Santha tilted her head back, savoring the sensation as the pain faded away and adrenaline surged through her. Her senses sharpened, and energy flashed through her in a seductive rush.

She grabbed a tourniquet from her pouch and yanked it tight around the top of her thigh. She ignored the ugly wound.

Then she ran.

She knew the stims wouldn't last long. She moved through buildings, ran along streets, leaped over abandoned cars. She needed as much distance between her and the aliens as she could get.

But the excited yips and snarls of canids were still following her.

They were tracking her.

She ran faster. Her lungs burned.

As she sprinted through what had once been a park, she rounded the now-overgrown playground where kids had once played and laughed. When had she last laughed? She knew. That last night with Kareena, before the fiery lights in the sky had turned night into day.

Santha burst out of the park and raced along the sidewalk. She rounded a corner and a huge wave of dizziness hit her.

No. No. The bracer was wearing off.

She staggered and hit a fence. Winded, she found her balance and kept moving. But her pace was slower now, her injured leg dragging behind her.

A huge explosion tore through the growing darkness.

The gas station.

Santha managed a small, satisfied smile. *Take that, you bastards.*

Pain filtered in. She gritted her teeth. *Have...to keep moving.* She looked down and saw her trouser leg was completely soaked in blood.

Santha forced herself to keep moving. One foot in front of the other. She was panting and sweat poured into her eyes. Sobbing, she pulled herself into an alley.

She couldn't go any farther.

Fumbling, she pulled a canister off her belt. It was a repellent she'd made that the canids hated. She opened it and dumped the contents on the ground. It wouldn't deter them for long, but it was better than nothing.

She moved farther into the alley, then dropped down behind a dumpster and dragged herself so her back was against the wall. She wasn't sure where she was exactly. How far to the top floor apartment with a view of the harbor that had become her home since the attack?

Her vision wavered and she closed her eyes.

Then she heard them.

The canids were coming.

She dropped her head back against the wall and

released a shuddering breath. "I'm so sorry, Kareena." Santha fumbled in her pocket and pulled out a photo. It was a shot of her and her sister, their arms around each other, laughing for the camera. Kareena was shorter and curvier than Santha—she took after their mother—and had a sunnier personality. She'd been the best of them, a nurse who'd loved caring for others. "Not going...to be able to take them all down for you, sis."

The canid snarls were much louder now.

Santha grabbed the last object on her belt. Another grenade.

Fighting off dizziness, she pulled the grenade close to her chest, her finger on the pin. She'd have to wait until the canids got really close. That way, she could take out as many as possible.

As she waited in the dark to die, her fuzzy thoughts turned to a handsome face and deep-brown eyes, and the regrets of what would never be.

Chapter Three

Cruz crept through the night, his night-vision lens showing everything around him in varying shades of green.

The team was moving behind him, everyone on alert for signs of the raptors.

Suddenly, an explosion ripped through the night. A ball of flames rose above the rooftops, flaring through his night vision. Behind him, he heard the others mutter curses.

Santha. Cruz waited for his eyes to adjust. It had to be.

He'd studied her movements on their drones over the last few weeks. She was a master at sneaking in, setting charges, and blowing raptors to hell.

Marcus moved up beside him. "Think it's her?"

"Yep."

"Let's check it out." Marcus waved the team on.

They moved fast now, sticking to the shadows. As they reached the explosion site, they crouched behind some abandoned cars and watched the chaos as raptors milled around a burning gas station. Two raptor armored personnel carriers were parked nearby—damned ugly, squat-looking things. There were plenty of raptor bodies lying on the ground as well, some burned beyond recognition.

Cruz smiled to himself. *Muy bien.* She was the queen of destruction.

Then he spied a few raptors through the flames who looked like they were arguing. Some were gesturing. Cruz grabbed his binocs. He waited for the view to zoom in and saw what they were pointing at. A small pack of canids were loping away.

Shit. "Canids are on the trail of something."

"Okay, Hell Squad," Marcus murmured. "Let's circle around these guys and see what's got the canids so excited."

They gave the raptors a wide berth, even though Cruz's fingers itched to take a few out. But first, he needed to find Santha.

The team moved away from the gas station and followed the canids. It was easy. The ugly beasts made a hell of a noise. He picked up a darker stain on the ground. Crouching, he pressed a finger to it and lifted.

Blood. "She's injured." Cruz broke into a lope. "We need to move faster."

Without comment, the team followed.

They moved through an overgrown park and back onto the street. Ahead, the canids gave some excited yips, heading for the mouth of an alley. They stopped there for a second and looked agitated.

Fuck. Cruz lifted his carbine, sighting the first

creature in his sights. He opened fire.

The canid went down. Seconds later, a barrage of laser fire tore into the rest of them as the squad did what they did best. Shaw managed to take down two with one shot. The sniper was magic with his rifle.

Soon a pile of canid bodies lay at the alley entrance.

Cruz moved forward, weapon aimed in case any of the canids were playing dead. Nothing moved. He smelled the faintest scent of green trees. He knew that smell—Santha's canid deterrent spray.

He stepped into the narrow space between two buildings. It was dark. A dumpster loomed in the shadows. He kept his steps slow, checking for any sign of movement. His heartbeat was loud in his ears.

Then he saw her slumped against the building. Her dark hair was a tangled mess covering her bent head.

Madre de dios. He hurried to her, dropping to his knees. "Santha?"

She lifted head, her eyelids fluttering open. "Cruz?" Her unfocused gaze hit his face. "Must...be dead."

"Not yet, *mi reina.*" He went to touch her and realized she was clutching a frag grenade to her chest. "Can I have this?"

Her fingers tightened on the pin. "Canids." A hoarse whisper.

"We took care of them. They're dead."

She blinked again, like she was trying to process

the information. He didn't think she even realized he was there. "Need to take out as many as I can."

His heart simply stopped.

She'd been planning to fucking blow herself up like a frigging sacrifice.

Anger was like a molten river storming through Cruz. He worked his jaw while he tried not to yell loud enough to bring raptors down on them.

Then he saw her thigh. He sucked in a breath. It was a mess. And the dark shadow beneath her wasn't muck or dirt...it was blood.

"She's hurt bad. Someone bring a med kit." He pressed a palm to her cheek. "Santha, the canids are dead. Give me the grenade and we'll get you out of here."

"Couldn't save Kareena. Regret...not getting revenge for her." Santha's eyelids drooped. "Regretted not kissing you."

Her last words were so quiet he barely heard them, but his heart kicked in his chest. He brushed the sweat-dampened hair off her head and pressed his lips to her ear. "You hold the fuck on, *mi reina*, and you'll get that kiss."

Now her eyes popped wide open. "Cruz? You're really here?"

"Yeah." He took the grenade from her loosened fingers, checked it, then stuck it through a loop on his belt.

"Thought you were a hallucination."

"Nope." He gently probed the wound on her thigh.

"Raptor poison," she said.

Cruz's jaw tightened. It had to hurt like hell. Gabe crouched beside him holding out an open med kit. Cruz nodded his thanks and snatched up a med-patch dressing. It would cauterize the wound and stop the bleeding for now. "She's lost a lot of blood."

"Want the nano-meds?" the other man asked.

It was a risk. The microscopic medical machines could heal her in only a few hours...but they had to be monitored by a medical professional, otherwise they could get out of control and kill the patient. The squad only used them when they had no other options.

Cruz finally shook his head. "They might kill her." He cupped her cheeks and forced her head up. "Think you can hold on until we get you somewhere safe?"

She managed a nod.

A muttered curse sounded in the darkness. Shaw called out from the roof above. "We have company incoming. Twenty raptors."

A second later, Elle's tense voice came through all their earpieces. "Actually, twenty-two."

Marcus stepped closer. "We can't take them on and protect Santha. Elle, you got a way out for us?"

"The raptors are between you and the Hawk. I'm working to find a safe route...but you'll have to go around."

Cruz slammed a fist into the ground. "She can't make it that long. We need somewhere to hole up and take care of her wound."

"Apartment." Santha grimaced. "Not far. Near

the harbor."

Cruz caught Marcus' gaze. "We can tend her there and wait out the raptors until it's safe to move."

Marcus pondered for a second, then nodded. "Okay, let's go. Elle, got that?"

"Got it. Be careful."

Marcus' teeth flashed white in the darkness. "Always."

Cruz crouched and slipped an arm around Santha's back. "I'm your ride, *mi reina*."

A faint smile flickered on her lips. "Not how I imagined riding you."

Cruz's cock went hard instantly, surging up against his body armor. "Hell, honey, stop that or I'm going to be in a world of pain." He lifted her into his arms. "I've got you now."

With a nod, she nestled her head against his shoulder, and for the first time since he'd met her, he felt her relax against him. "Sorry, I'm too tall to be light."

"I could tell you all about my manly strength, but my armor has an exoskeleton. You're as light as a feather."

That small smile appeared again.

Hell Squad moved steadily through the night. Santha hadn't lost consciousness but her lethargy and pale face had a tight feeling growing in his gut. She whispered directions through dry lips.

"More raptors incoming," Gabe said, staring through the scope on his carbine. "Streets are crawling with them."

Cruz cursed. "They're hunting us."

Elle's voice broke through. "You're right. And I see two more patrols heading to your area. You need to hide. Now!"

"We have to get to Santha's place, people. Go!" Marcus said.

A few times they had to take cover and wait for raptor patrols to pass. Because she didn't make a single noise, the only way Cruz knew Santha was hurting was by the way her hand gripped his armor.

Finally, she pointed to a half-destroyed apartment building, maybe twenty stories high. It was on the water, and would have cost a small fortune in the days before the invasion. He suspected back in the day, it had a magnificent view of the harbor.

"Seventeenth floor," she said. "Take the stairs on the southern side."

Cruz got a better view of the building and ground his teeth together. Half the fucking building was gone. Who knew if it was stable? It could come crashing down around her any second.

She wasn't staying here any longer. Even if he had to drag her out of here fighting and screaming, he was taking her back to base with him.

They reached the outer door leading to the stairwell. It was blocked, covered by debris and a trailer piled with old furniture.

"Give the trailer a push," she said.

Gabe did and the trailer moved easily so they could open the door.

"Clever," Cruz said.

"There are some booby traps in the stairs, too. Didn't want anyone sneaking up on me."

The stairwell was pitch-black, but with their night-vision gear, they made quick work of moving upward and dodging the ingenious booby traps she'd rigged. She pointed out the steps she'd rigged to fall away under body weight, empty soda cans that hid grenades and the tripwires that doused the stairs with buckets of the substance she'd developed that repelled the canids.

Shaw slid past a small pile of disguised grenades. "Hell. You are bloodthirsty, woman."

Santha shot him a cool look. "Smart."

Cruz swallowed a smile, shifted her higher in his arms and stepped carefully over the grenades.

On the seventeenth floor, she pointed to a door half-way along the hallway. But Cruz was too busy staring at the end of the hall, where walls no longer existed, and he could see out into open space. *Dammit to hell.*

Santha handed over a set of keys and Cruz passed them to Marcus. There were three heavy locks and Marcus opened each one.

Marcus and Claudia went first to clear the apartment. At Marcus' nod, Cruz moved inside. The apartment had probably been luxurious once. Now Santha had boarded up the windows, but in a way not to draw any attention from the outside. She'd shoved furniture aside and had stockpiled what looked like canned food, weapons, ammunition and medical supplies against the wall.

One couch faced the spacious kitchen and Cruz set her down on it.

"Let's take a look at that wound."

Shaw kneeled beside Cruz with a med kit. The rest of the squad were patrolling the space, checking exits, weapons still up and on alert.

Cruz tore the blood-soaked fabric away from her thigh. The wound made him wince. The raptor poison had made a damned mess. But what worried him most was that it was still bleeding.

He grabbed some sterile wipes from Shaw and set to work cleaning it. "Don't know how you're still conscious. The pain or paralysis should have taken you out."

She leaned her head back against the cushions. "Took a bracer to get away from the canids."

Cruz froze, Shaw and Marcus cursed and Claudia hissed in a breath.

"How long ago, Santha?" Cruz asked.

Her head lolled against the couch. "It wore off before you found me."

Fuck. Too long. "It's numbed your pain and kept you functioning." And masked just how badly injured she was. He checked her pulse the old-fashioned way, fingers to wrist. Weak and erratic. He snatched up a pen light and shined it in her eyes.

Her pupils didn't respond.

"Fuck. It's bad, and she's lost too much blood."

"Nano-meds," Marcus said.

They could kill her but they had no choice. Cruz nodded to Shaw, who fished in the med kit. "She'll still need blood."

"You know we don't carry any," Shaw said.

"But we have a field transfusion kit, right?"

Shaw frowned. "Yeah."

Cruz held out his arm. "Hook me up. Give her my blood."

Shaw glanced at Marcus. Cruz didn't bother to look at his friend.

"Do it," Marcus said.

Shaw nodded and snapped on some thin gloves. First, he pulled out a large syringe filled with a glittering, silver fluid that shifted and moved. Cruz gripped Santha's shoulders and held her down. He knew from experience that the nano-meds hurt like hell.

Shaw slid the needle into her vein and injected the nanos.

For a second, nothing happened, then Santha's body bowed up and a strangled sound ripped from her throat.

"It's okay, *mi reina*, I know it hurts. Only for a little while."

She pressed against him. "Burns."

"Yeah, those little bugs are burrowing in, spreading through your blood stream. They're gonna fix you up."

Shaw pressed a tiny sensor to the side of her neck. A light on it blinked crazily. He lifted a small tablet. "I'll monitor her vitals here and check the nanos' progress."

He could pull them back if they got too aggressive or speed them up. What they couldn't do was turn them off. Now they were in, they had to run their course. And nano-meds, not properly monitored, could kill quicker than a raptor mortar.

Santha finally relaxed against the cushions, her body drenched in sweat. Cruz brushed her hair off her face. Was shocked to see his hand wasn't entirely steady.

He settled on the floor beside her and took off his upper-body armor. He held out his arm. "Ready?"

Shaw nodded and wrapped a rubber tourniquet around Cruz's bicep. As Shaw sank the needle into the crook of Cruz's arm, Cruz didn't wince, he just kept his gaze on Santha's still face. Shaw finished connecting the thin tube between Cruz, the tiny, high-tech field transfusion machine, and Santha. Bright-red blood flowed, filling the tube. It passed through the trans machine and into Santha.

It took some time. Cruz watched her face, studying her high cheekbones, bronze skin and her long, dark lashes. He saw a scar on the side of her neck slowly losing the pink freshness of a recent wound. She'd been hurt some time in the last few months. His fingers curled into a fist. He imagined her lying here, in pain, bleeding, alone.

"Cruz?"

Her voice snapped him out of his angry contemplation. Her face had more color and her eyes were focused on his face.

"Feeling better?"

"Yes." She eyed the blood flowing into her. "Your blood must pack a punch." She stirred. "Can you help me sit up?"

He slid onto the couch next to her and helped her sit.

With a shaky hand, she brushed her hair back. "Dammit. I hate feeling like this."

Yeah, feeling weak sucked. "You'll be back on your feet soon."

She eyed her neatly dressed thigh. "Nano-meds, right? I've only healed this quickly once before."

"We carry a dose. Emergencies only." Cruz nodded to Shaw. "Shaw here is monitoring them so they don't decide to eat your insides."

Shaw leaned forward. "Right now they're mending the sources of your bleeding. They've already eradicated the raptor poison from your system. Won't have enough oomph to fix the exterior and close the wound, but Doc Emerson will solve that."

"Doc Emerson?"

Cruz nodded. "Dr. Emerson Green. She's in charge of the medical teams at Blue Mountain Base."

Santha tried to straighten. "I'm not leaving—"

"Yes, you are." Cruz pressed his palms to the couch back on either side of her head. "I'm not taking no for an answer this time, Santha. You were hurt, nearly died, and you live in a fucking ruin that could tumble down any second. You are coming back to base."

"You think you have a say in my life?" she spat.

"Yeah."

She leaned forward until their noses brushed.

"No. I don't even give my lovers that power."

"Well, I'm gonna be your lover soon enough and I'm also the man who wants you fucking safe, *comprende?*"

Marcus cleared his throat. "Cruz's...arguments aside, we need your help, Santha."

She stared at Cruz a second more before her gaze flicked to Marcus. "Help?"

"Raptors are keeping human prisoners somewhere in the city, including some pretty valuable scientists," Marcus said.

Her green gaze moved back to Cruz.

He nodded. "The powers that be want them all out of raptor hands, but we don't know where they are."

She released a slow breath. "What do you need?"

"Intel. Raptor locations, numbers, anything you've seen that might lead to where these prisoners are being held."

She gave a slow nod. "I haven't seen any human prisoners. Everyone I've seen caught is usually killed, not taken prisoner. But I have locations and can probably narrow it down to the best possibilities."

"That would help a lot," Marcus said.

Shaw leaned forward to detach the transfusion device from Cruz and Santha's arms. When she struggled to get up off the couch, Cruz slid an arm around her and took most of her weight.

She shot him an unfriendly look but didn't protest. "Come on. I'll show you my data."

Chapter Four

Santha hobbled across the living room, horribly aware that the only thing keeping her upright was Cruz. Without his armor on, the warmth of his hard body blasted through her. The man was so incredibly hot.

In more ways than one.

She pushed that thought aside. He was also an alpha warrior used to getting his own way. She didn't need that distraction in her life. Right now, they had some prisoners to focus on.

All of the possible reasons the raptors might be keeping human prisoners cascaded through her head. None of them were good.

She opened the door to one of the bedrooms and Cruz reached out an arm to push it open wider. With only a black T-shirt stretched over his chest, his arms were bare and striking black ink in a fascinating tribal design peeked out from beneath the edges of the sleeves. She eyed the way it wrapped around his muscled biceps. Her fingers twitched. *No touching.* But it did make her wonder what other ink he might have on that fascinating body.

She cleared her throat. "There's a battery-powered lantern on the table. The windows are blacked out."

He reached past her and flicked it on. It filled the room with a muted, blue light.

The rest of Cruz's team pushed in behind them.

"Holy hell," Claudia breathed.

Shaw was blinking, his gaze glued to the wall. "You're right, you are smart."

The entire wall was filled with her recon information. Maps, notes, photos. Things were grouped in clusters and she'd drawn lines with dark marker on the wall linking various items. Her gaze fell on one familiar photo, containing a tall, lean raptor with smoother, darker skin.

Marcus approached the wall, fingering a picture showing raptor ships landing in a park. "How long have you been putting this together?"

"Pretty much since the bastards arrived." Since the day after she'd watched, helpless, as they'd dragged her sister's dead body away.

"And this?" Gabe had nudged open the adjoining door. The bathroom was packed with lab equipment, glass beakers with tubes running from one to another. A pale-green fluid filled them.

"That's where I make the cedar oil substance that repels the canids."

Cruz's arm tightened on her. She'd given them the recipe for the spray a few weeks back and the geek squad back at base were busy replicating it. "We need you to come to base. We'll bring all this with us. After the doc gives you the all-clear, we need your help to plan out the recon missions to find the prisoners."

Santha didn't hesitate. "Okay."

He cocked his head. "Just like that? When you were ready to fight me before?"

"They killed my sister. Those prisoners, they're someone else's sisters, brothers, lovers. I'll do whatever I can to help you free them."

Suddenly, an intense wave of cold washed over her. She shivered and her knees gave way like they were made of wet rope. With a curse, Cruz caught her.

Shaw swore. "Nanos are getting a bit aggressive." The sniper tapped his tablet screen.

Giant shivers wracked Santha, her teeth chattering so hard she thought they'd shatter. God, it hurt.

Cruz swept her up into his arms. "Shaw?"

"Fuck. Fuck!" Shaw looked up. "Cascade."

Now, Cruz swore. Gritting her teeth through the pain, she looked up at him. "What...is...it?"

"The nano-meds are out of control. If we don't get you back to base...they'll kill you."

Marcus stepped forward. "You two keep Santha as comfortable as possible. Claudia, you bag Santha's data. Gabe, contact Elle and call in a Hawk for pick up."

"There are raptors everywhere," Gabe said. "It won't be safe for a Hawk to land."

"Roof," Santha forced out.

Cruz nodded, hauling her closer. "Right, have them land on the roof. We'll need to set some flares to guide them in."

Gabe nodded and rushed out.

After that, everything seemed to move at double speed. Shaw pumped Santha full of some sort of sedative that left her feeling like she was floating. She still felt the painful cold, she just didn't give a crap about it. She curled into Cruz's warmth, enjoying the way he kept stroking her back.

"Got everything." Claudia came back to the living room, two bulging backpacks slung over each shoulder.

"Hawk's en route," Gabe announced. "They want to do a hot extraction. They'll get close enough for us to jump aboard but won't land."

"That'll do." Marcus hefted his carbine. "Hell Squad, let's hit the roof. Ready to go to hell?"

"Hell, yeah!" they all responded. "The devil needs an ass-kicking!"

They headed up the stairs, their boots pounding on the steps. They burst out onto the rooftop.

Gabe and Marcus hurried to set the laser flares on the edge of the roof. Santha just watched in a daze. It was strange to have spent a year alone, with barely any human contact, and now be surrounded by this intense team of soldiers.

Marcus touched his ear. "Elle says the Hawk's almost here."

Santha frowned. Illusion systems couldn't hide lights, and she didn't see any lights in the sky. They wouldn't come in with lights blazing for the raptors to see, but it took a damn good pilot with a big set of balls to fly into the city in the dark.

Sure enough, the dark shape of the quadcopter

appeared out of the darkness above them, flying silently, as it ran on a tiny thermonuclear engine and the rotors were shrouded to reduce their noise. The men ignited the laser flares and neon-green light speared upward. The Hawk adjusted course and headed straight for them.

She watched the Hawk's rotors tilt and the Hawk descended. About a meter above the roof, it stopped and hovered. Marcus leaped up onto the skids, yanking the door open.

Cruz handed Santha to Marcus. The rest of the team leaped aboard, moving to positions by the doors, guns raised. Gabe climbed into the seat of a fixed autocannon.

Cruz settled in a seat and Marcus handed Santha back over. She looked up at Cruz.

"Why am I in your lap?"

"I like you there, *mi reina*."

"When I'm not feeling as high as a supersonic jet, I'll probably be pissed about this."

He smiled and damned if that trademark grin of his didn't make his sexy face even sexier.

"In case you haven't realized," he drawled, "I get turned on when you're pissed at me."

A laugh burst from her. "You're crazy."

Suddenly a shout came from the cockpit and the entire team tensed.

"Incoming raptor ptero," the pilot yelled. "Everyone hold on!"

***

Cruz had just finished tightening the safety strap around himself and Santha when the Hawk veered sharply to the left.

"Ptero?" Santha asked.

"It's what we call their ships."

The Hawk veered again.

Shaw slammed into the wall, Claudia was cursing.

Gabe let loose with the autocannon, sending bursts of green laser fire spitting out into the night.

Cruz tightened his arms around Santha and craned his neck to see through to the cockpit.

Finn—Hawk pilot extraordinaire—sat in the pilot's seat, his hands doing a frantic dance across the controls. Through the cockpit window, Cruz saw the bright-red lights of two raptor pteros. The ships looked like giant pterosaurs, with two large, fixed wings sharpening to a pointed cockpit at front, and a long, tail-like back end.

Suddenly, Finn threw the Hawk into evasive maneuvers. "Hold on! They're firing that damn poison. Chews right through metal," he yelled.

Marcus gripped a bar on the roof to stay upright. "Swing us around so Gabe can get a shot."

The Hawk turned fast. Gabe fired.

Cruz felt Santha's fingers digging into his arm. Looking down, he saw the lines bracketing her mouth. She wasn't doing well. They needed to get back to base...now.

"Don't worry, Finn here is the best Hawk pilot we have. He'll get us back to base."

Raptor fire hit the side of the Hawk, jolting

them. The metal hissed and sizzled as the acidic substance ate through it. Sparks flew from a side console and Marcus cursed. He snatched up a fire extinguisher and covered the raptor poison in foam.

"Sorry," Finn called back.

Cruz watched as the Hawk speared west, dodging the fire from their pursuers.

The two raptor pteros pulled in on either side of the Hawk. Gabe swung the turret and opened fire with another lethal barrage of laser fire.

The ptero lurched to the side, one of its wings pointing straight down. Then it fell into death spiral, plummeting earthward.

"Woo-hoo, great shootin', Tex," Shaw called out. "My turn now."

The sniper stood on the other side of the copter, his laser rifle pointed out a small window. He fired.

Laser fire hit the small window on the ptero cockpit. The alien ship shuddered and fell back. But it wasn't stopping its pursuit.

Cruz tapped his fingers on the armrest. They had to lose the ptero. They couldn't risk exposing the location of Blue Mountain Base.

Santha shifted. "Weak spot."

"What?" Cruz asked.

"I've spent a lot of time watching them." She pulled in a breath like it took a lot of effort. Her face was so pale. "Small intake where the wing meets the body. I've experimented shooting a crossbow bolt in there and it brings them down. Every time."

"Shaw? You hear that?"

47

"Yep." Shaw was sighting his rifle again. "How come we didn't know this?"

"Well, we do now," Marcus said. "Can you see it?"

"Yep." Shaw raised his voice. "Hey, fly boy, can you keep this thing still for a second?"

"You come up here and fly it, asshole," came the reply.

Shaw snorted. "Only if you come back here and shoot this fucker out of the sky." Then his face changed, evened out, as he focused on his high-tech scope.

"Take the shot," Marcus said.

Shaw fired.

Cruz saw the ptero explode into flames.

"Yeah, baby!" Shaw yelled.

Claudia was grinning. Gabe clapped Shaw on the back, and Cruz smiled.

Until he heard Santha's quiet groan. Her shaking was worse. He pulled her closer. "Hold on, *mi reina*, almost there."

"*Mi reina*. What's it mean?"

He brushed a thumb over her cheek. "My queen."

She opened her eyes and he sucked in a breath. Her pale-green irises were gone, replaced by a metallic silver. The bugs were replicating too fast.

Suddenly, her back arched and she started convulsing.

No, no, he couldn't lose her.

"Finn, hurry!" Cruz unstrapped the harness and laid her on the floor. "Hang in there, Santha."

Her convulsions continued and, helpless, all he could do was hold her hand.

He leaned down and put his mouth against her ear. "Fight, dammit. You've been fighting every day since these bastards came. Don't you fucking die now."

***

Santha felt like she was drifting in a fog. Her vision was blurred, but she had impressions of dark shadows and bright lights. Cruz's deep, accented voice was in the background, talking to her, telling her to hold on. Her body was so cold, she'd lost all sensation.

Then nothing.

When she woke, she stared up at bright track lights running across a smooth, concrete-lined ceiling. Under her, was a bed made up with crisp sheets.

She sat up, the white sheet sliding off her. She was dressed only in a medical gown and panties. Turning her head, she noted the rows of similar, narrow beds. Infirmary.

Lifting the sheet, she quickly pulled up the gown to bare her thigh.

Nothing to see, except smooth, slightly-pink new skin. She rubbed the faint scar and knew in a month or two it wouldn't even be visible.

"You're awake."

A pretty blonde woman in a white coat bustled around the bed. Her hair fell in a neat bob around her face.

"Ah...yes."

The woman smiled. "I'm Dr. Emerson Green. Everyone calls me Doc, or just Emerson." She peered at the tablet she carried. "Your vitals are looking good. We weren't sure you were going to pull through the nano-med cascade. The bugs had gone to town on your insides." She set the tablet aside and pulled a slim m-scanner from her front pocket. "But being the medical genius I am, you're now perfectly healthy."

Santha watched as the woman checked her leg. "Thank you. I actually haven't felt this good in...well, a long time."

Emerson smiled. "Glad to hear it. Those nano-meds would have fixed anything they found—injury, malnutrition, exhaustion." She slipped the m-scanner away. "Now, I'm going to tell Cruz he can come in. I banished him to the hall and he's been pacing out there impatiently for—" she checked her watch "—three hours."

Santha settled back on the pillows and watched Cruz stride toward her. He looked...angry.

He stopped beside her bed, looming there like a statue. He'd showered and his dark hair was damp. She'd never seen him in anything other than his battle gear. Cruz Ramos in faded jeans and a black T-shirt was...heart-stoppingly delicious.

"You're feeling better?" he said with a scowl.

"Good as new, according to the doctor."

He pressed his hands to the side of the bed. "What the fuck were you doing?"

Santha narrowed her gaze. "Excuse me?"

"Bombing that raptor supply depot, making yourself a big fat target for the canids."

She lowered her voice. "I warned you about the alpha asshole tactics, Cruz. I won't have it. I was fighting the aliens who are destroying our planet."

"You almost died! You would have blown yourself up in that dirty, fucking alley."

"Yes."

Something dangerous flashed in his eyes. "You died in my arms on the way to the infirmary!" He spun away, lifting his arms and putting his hands behind his head. "Luckily, Doc Emerson revived you."

Santha watched his taut back. He was so tense he looked like he might snap. She swung her legs over the side of the bed. Damn, it was so good not to have to take days to recover. The nano-meds, for all their trying to kill her, had done their job and left her feeling one hundred percent.

"I'm fine, Cruz. Perfectly healthy and alive."

His arms dropped to his sides.

She stood and walked up behind him. She pressed a palm to the center of his back and his head fell forward. "Why does it matter to you if I die?"

He stayed silent.

"You barely know me," she said quietly.

He pulled in a breath. "You fight, you're tough and smart, and sexy as hell. What's not to like?"

Santha trembled. God, just a few simple words and he could bring her to her knees.

"I've never met anyone like you and I know you feel it," he continued. "This…connection between us."

Dammit, she did. But she shouldn't. Revenge was all she had room for.

"The first time I saw you was like a damn lightning bolt."

She closed her eyes and allowed herself a second to absorb the pleasure of his words. "Caring about people leads to hurt and pain."

"Bullshit." He spun, grabbing her hands. "It doesn't have to."

"In this new world, the raptors will destroy anything you care about." She was pressed against that hard chest and all the vital warmth of him. He was so painfully alive and she'd felt so cold and alone for so long.

He lowered his head, his lips just a centimeter from hers. "There can be pleasure as well."

Santha had attacked raptors twice her size and escaped packs of canids more times than she could count.

But now her pulse was racing faster and her mouth was drier than when any raptor had been after her.

"Well, where's all that crazy courage of yours now?" he murmured.

Chapter Five

That taunt and the burning look in Cruz's chocolate-brown eyes ignited something in Santha. She pressed her hand to his rock-hard chest and shoved him. He went back a step and then she leaped at him.

Her mouth crashed against his but he was already moving to meet her. She thrust her tongue into his mouth, plastering herself against him. With a groan, Cruz wrapped his arms around her and spun. They smacked into the wall and he pinned her there.

God, he tasted so good. Something in her snapped. She hadn't touched another human being in over a year. She was tired of being alone. Tired of being strong all the time. She poured everything she had into the kiss. All her loneliness, fear, grief. But also her desire, her secret wants, all the times she'd watched him from afar. All the times she'd fantasized about his hard warrior's body.

Her nails scored his shoulders and she tried to climb up him, to get closer. His hand gripped her thigh and pulled it around his hip. He ground his very hard erection against her and her cry was swallowed by his mouth.

So. Good. Santha stroked her tongue against his. Her nipples were so hard they hurt and she was wet and aching between her legs. She wanted him. More than she'd wanted anything in her life.

Then he pulled back. He rested his forehead on hers, panting a little.

Santha struggled to get her brain working and get air into her burning lungs. She wanted to drag him down on the floor and tear those jeans off and see if his cock was as thick as she imagined. "Why are we stopping?"

"You were hurt. I shouldn't be pawing you like this."

She raised a brow. "The bugs fixed me better than I was before. I'm perfectly healthy." She moved her hips against him to make the point. And okay, she liked teasing him. His groan was music to her ears.

"But mentally, you need time." He stepped back, winced and adjusted his jeans. "Come on, I'll give you a tour of base."

Santha stared at him and stayed where she was. Mainly because she needed the wall to hold her up until her legs stopped feeling like jelly. She was stuck between feeling mad he'd stopped and feeling pleasure that he was looking after her. Again.

Finally, she straightened. "I'd prefer we get naked—"

He groaned again.

Oh, yeah, the evil part of her liked that sound.

"But if you're too busy being noble and that isn't an option then I'd like to get straight to work planning the recon missions."

"Tour on the way to work." He gestured to a folded pile of clothes on the next bed. "I found some stuff for you to wear. Hopefully it fits."

After Santha changed into the plain black trousers, simple T-shirt the color of wine, and some canvas shoes—all of which fitted her perfectly, attesting to Cruz's experience sizing up women— she walked alongside him as they wandered the tunnels of the base. It was early morning and lots of people bustled around, starting their day. Despite the bare-concrete walls and the industrial look, she was surprised that the place felt almost...cozy.

He showed her the dining room and adjoining rec room. Someone had found old movie posters and hung them on the wall beside a huge projection screen. The other side of the room had a line of impressive high-tech games. In one corner, she spotted a guitar leaning against the wall, along with some other instruments. Above them, someone had taped a photo of Cruz playing guitar.

She moved closer. He looked so...lost in the playing. He leaned over the guitar, holding it like he might a woman, his eyes closed.

She glanced over her shoulder. "You play?"

He shrugged and looked away. "Yeah. But I haven't been playing much lately." He headed for the doorway. "Let's keep going."

Lots of people called out to Cruz. She noted

everyone looked at him with respect...and some with a little awe. And many of the women watched him with feminine appreciation...and some, outright hunger.

Santha's stomach clenched. How many of them were his regular playmates? How many knew the feel of those hard muscles, had traced those sexy tattoos with their tongues?

"The school's through here."

His voice snapped her out of her unpleasant thoughts. It was none of her business who he slept with. And if she decided to play with him, well, she only wanted something hard and fast and temporary, so it didn't matter. She followed him into another tunnel.

They walked past a few rooms with doors wide open. Inside were bunches of kids of differing ages. In the first, solemn teenagers hunched over tablets. A boy noticed them and waved at Cruz.

Cruz lifted a hand. "Leo and his girlfriend were living in those train tunnels near the airport. We rescued them after that mission to destroy the raptor comms hub."

"Can the base hold many more survivors?"

They passed the next room. Tiny kids were bouncing around, squealing and giggling. Bright, hand-painted pictures graced the walls. Santha couldn't help but smile at their simple joy. They didn't seem worried about an alien apocalypse.

"We have about a thousand living here, and there's room yet," Cruz answered. "A lot of tunnels are still closed up or being used for storage. We stockpile any supplies we're able to scavenge, and also store any art or valuables we've rescued for safekeeping."

Santha wondered how many of the humanity's treasures had been annihilated by the raptors.

"There's also a hydroponics garden for growing food, and research areas where the scientist work on projects like power, weaponry and medicine. And just up ahead is geek land, also known as the comp lab. Noah Kim's our resident genius. He's responsible for all our comms systems and our drones."

"I've never seen any of your drones."

"They aren't big enough to be noticeable. After the raptors destroyed all the satellites, we had to find another way to get imaging and intel." His face turned grim. "We lost a lot of good soldiers in the first few months because of a lack of intel. After the attack, Noah spearheaded the project to adapt small experimental drones to take high-res images and feed them back to base."

"Amazing."

"Here we are." Cruz stopped at a door with a sign hanging on it that said, *Shh, genius at work.*

She raised a brow. "Humble, is he?"

"Noah'll just tell you he's stating a fact. Guy's not afraid to tell it how it is." Cruz pushed open the door.

Santha stepped inside. "Whoa." There were bits of electronic...stuff...everywhere. Benches lined one wall and were overflowing with computer parts, tools and wiring. There were a few battered metal desks with huge comp screens on them, and people working hard at them.

At one desk, a good-looking man wearing glasses looked up. He had some Asian heritage and midnight eyes in a lean face with high cheekbones. They were making genius computer geeks well these days. She didn't know if he wore his dark hair long by design or he'd just forgotten to get it cut, but he'd tied it back at the base of his neck, giving him a rakish look.

"Hey, Noah," Cruz said.

"Cruz. Who's your friend?"

"Santha Kade, this is Noah Kim. He and his team keep the lights on and the power running. Wish you'd do something about the hot water, though. A few hours a day isn't enough."

Noah snorted. "It's on my list. Along with the five hundred other things we need. Once I can squeeze some more power out of the solar panels, I'll..." he drifted off and offered Santha a wry grin. "Sorry, I have a bad habit of going into details these grunts never want to hear about."

She wandered closer. "Cruz was telling me they're lucky to have you. You repurposed the drones."

"Yep." He opened a drawer, pulled out something the size of his hand and set it on his desk. "This one's in for maintenance. Had a nasty run-in with a bird."

Santha picked it up. It looked a bit like a miniature Hawk with four rotors. "It's so small."

"All the better for the raptors not to notice them.

And I've rigged them with illusion systems."

She set it down. "What did you do…before the raptors came?"

"Worked in R and D for a private tech company." He grinned. "And ran my own online company. Made my first billion by the time I hit twenty-five."

Cruz made a scoffing sound. "Billions don't matter anymore, boy genius."

Noah gave him the finger. "What do you do, Santha?"

"I kill raptors."

He raised a brow. "Well, you're in good company. Cruz and his Hell Squad buddies are the best at that."

She caught Cruz's gaze. "Yeah, I know." She looked away and spied a row of dice on a shelf. "These are great." She reached out for the closest one—it looked old and made of green glass.

"I wouldn't touch those if I were you, or you're likely to end up with the ventilation in your room mysteriously not working," Cruz said.

She snatched her hand back.

Noah smiled. "My collection. I don't let anyone touch them except me." His smiled dissolved. "Only thing I brought with me from…before."

Santha thought of the picture of Kareena tucked in her pocket. "I know the feeling."

Noah talked a few more minutes about the base's computer systems before Cruz pulled her out of the lab.

"Guy'll talk your ear off about computers."

"What's up next on the tour?"

"The Operations Area. Where all the military operations are run from. The drone operators are based there, as well as the communications officers who provide comms to each squad in the field. Ours is Elle. She's magic."

Santha heard a warmth in his voice and remembered the woman who'd been with them on the mission in the airport train tunnels. "She's with Marcus, right?"

Cruz smiled. "Oh, yeah. Has the big guy wrapped around her elegant little finger."

Santha smiled, too. "And you're happy about that."

"Yeah. Marcus is one of the best men I know. He deserved some happiness."

Santha's smile evaporated. And that stuff was in short supply these days.

He showed her to a secured door marked "Operations." He pressed a palm to an electronic lock. It beeped, and the door retracted.

Inside, was a large room with rows of drone operators in front of live-feed screens and uniformed people hurrying between computer terminals.

"We call that the Hive." He led her to another room off the main tunnel. "We're in here."

Inside, more large screens lined the wall, each one filled with aerial images of the city. All her research had been stuck to the walls, recreated almost perfectly.

Hell Squad lounged around the room.

Marcus stepped forward. "You look better."

Santha nodded. "I feel better. Thanks for getting me out."

Shaw sauntered forward with a smile. "Anytime you need a team to go into hell, we're there." He touched a finger to her chin. "You look really good."

Cruz made a growling sound. "Back off, Baird."

Shaw lifted his hands, his face filled with mock fear.

Santha fought off a smile. "Good shooting with that ptero."

The sniper gave a little bow. "I've been blessed with several skills." He waggled his eyebrows. "If you ever want to shake Neanderthal man here, I'll show you what else I'm good at."

Claudia made a gagging noise from where she leaned against the wall. "God, you'll hit on anything and anyone, won't you."

Shaw ran his tongue over his teeth and winked at Santha. "Just the pretty ones, Frost. And the nice ones, which is why you're excluded."

Claudia made a rude sound and shot him the finger.

Someone cleared their throat and Santha looked over at the man in front of the screens. He was a little older than her and carried an air of authority and command. He had a handsome face, like movie-star handsome, and a dash of gray at his temples that suited him. His khaki uniform was pressed and neat.

"I'm General Adam Holmes." He rounded the conference table. "I'm very happy to see you've recovered."

Ah, the boss. "Santha Kade and I'm pretty happy I recovered, too." The general held out a hand and they shook. He had a firmer grip than she would have guessed. Behind her, she felt Cruz step up close to her. She resisted rolling her eyes. He should just beat his chest and toss her over his shoulder.

"Thank you for sharing your intelligence with us," Holmes said. "The sooner we can locate and rescue these prisoners the better."

There was a sharp edge to his voice that made her study him again. She got the impression Holmes could be just as dangerous as the Hell Squad members in the right situation. And she suspected plenty of people underestimated him, blinded by his neat façade.

"Then let's get to work," she said.

They all settled into the chairs around the table, gazes on the big screen. A pretty brunette handed Santha a handheld comp controller with a smile. "I've scanned as much of your data into the comp as I could."

"Thanks. It's Elle, right?"

"That's right." She gestured to the screen. "Everything's in the directory marked Santha."

Santha studied the list of files and pulled up her maps.

Holmes leaned forward. "You have incredible data. And you've survived in the city alone for a year, attacking the raptors and assisting Squad Six."

Squad Six? She blinked. Right, that must be

Hell Squad's official designation.

Shrewd blue eyes watched her. "I take it you weren't a schoolteacher or business executive before the invasion."

She gave a wry smile. "No." She glanced at Cruz. "I was a police officer. With SWAT."

Cruz nodded. "Makes sense. You have the skills and training, knowledge of the city...and the guts."

God, she felt so flattered by his words. Like some schoolgirl. She turned back to the screen. "I'll start with the main raptor installations. I haven't quite determined what they all are yet, but some are clearly for storage, some are bases where they appear to live and work, others are complete mysteries. I can only guess some of them are research stations where they gather data on us and the planet. Possibly, they're carrying out tests on our technology and resources."

"We've seen that they're studying our languages, trying to decipher our books, files and scientific information," Elle said.

Santha nodded. "It's what I'd do if I ever invaded someone. Let me show you a few locations that seem larger and more well-used. I'm guessing that's where they're more likely to hold prisoners."

They clicked through maps, everyone calling out theories and suggestions. Elle was furiously taking notes on a tablet. They narrowed down a long list of possibilities.

"I'll move onto the aliens themselves." Santha pulled up her photos.

"I've been working on their language," Elle said.

"They call themselves the Gizzida."

"Ugly name for an ugly species." Santha pointed to the screen. "You're familiar with the main fighter raptors. We also have the rexes." Santha didn't hide her distaste as she stared at the picture of the giant T-Rex-type alien. "Thankfully, there seem to be only a few of those. The canids." Another two images appeared—a picture of a canid pack and a close-up of one roaring. "And you saw the hellion canids in the airport train tunnels." The image changed to one of the mutant canids with red, glowing bellies filled with an acidic poison.

"Hell Squad told me the canid repellent spray we're creating now came from you," Holmes said.

"Yes. It's based on cedar oil, which is toxic to reptiles. I tried a lot of things to see if anything repelled them and this seems to work. It won't kill them or stop them for long, but they don't like it."

"We're starting field tests soon, so thank you."

She nodded. "I also took these pictures very recently." It showed raptors moving an enclosed box the size of a car. "It was rocking violently and I could hear snarling."

"Another type of alien?" Holmes said with a frown.

"I think so. But I never got to see it."

"How many boxes like that?" Cruz asked.

"About a dozen. And the raptors seemed nervous. Didn't like dealing with them."

Shaw flopped back in his chair. "Great. Why do I get the impression we do *not* want to know what's in that box?"

"We've also seen a very large raptor," Cruz said. "A super-raptor. He carried a flamethrower and spoke some English."

Santha nodded. "I've seen one but didn't get any images of it. I called it a flamer."

"Works for me," Cruz said.

Santha clicked up another image and watched everyone frown.

"That's just another raptor," Cruz said.

"Look again." Staring at the commander's face made Santha's blood boil.

"It's taller and leaner than the other raptors," Elle said.

"Good. You'll also note the smoother skin that's several shades darker than a regular raptor."

"Still looks like a raptor to me," Claudia said.

"It is. But I also think it's a female raptor," Santha said.

Everyone hissed in breaths.

"A female?" Holmes repeated.

"Yes. And she appears to be the one in charge in this area. The commander." Santha caught Cruz's gaze. He was watching her intently. "And I want her dead."

Chapter Six

Cruz could almost feel the rage pumping off Santha. "Why? Why do you want this one dead so badly?"

"She's in charge of destroying our part of the world. Our city!"

He studied the stark lines of Santha's face. "That's true. But it's more than that, isn't it?"

"She killed my sister."

He saw the way Santha's hands curled into fists. She was barely hanging on. "You saw?"

"Every second." Her eyes squeezed shut. "It was about a week after the invasion. A raptor patrol caught us in the street. I fought, but got a tiny splatter of their fucking poison on me. I couldn't move, couldn't even speak and got tossed by a raptor. I ended up under a car." She dragged in a breath. "They beat my sister to death and there wasn't a single thing I could do about it."

Madre de dios. Cruz closed his eyes for a second. He knew what it felt like to watch someone you cared about die. They'd all been there when Zeke had fallen. But at least they'd been fighting back.

"They didn't even leave me a body to bury." Her green gaze caught Cruz's, glimmering with unshed tears. "They dragged her away like trash and the commander just stood there like she was watching a mildly inferior show."

He wanted to touch her, but he was afraid she'd shatter. To see a strong woman's tears almost bought him to his knees. "I'm sorry. We'll help you avenge your sister."

"Wait a minute," Holmes said. "We can't have personal vendettas—"

"We'll help you find this raptor commander and kill her," Marcus reiterated.

Holmes pinched the bridge of his nose. "Steele, I do not want to have another shouting match with you about the chain of command."

"Don't stress, Holmes," Marcus growled. "We'll get the prisoners too."

Elle cleared her throat to ease the tension. "I'm so sorry, Santha. I've no doubt this information can help us beat the raptors."

Santha wiped a hand across her face and straightened. "I hope so."

Elle's considering gaze moved back to the screen and the picture of the commander. "They're a bit like a bee colony."

"What?" Cruz asked, frowning.

"There are thousands of raptor fighters, they're kind of like worker bees."

"And this commander is like the queen?" Claudia asked.

"I don't know." Elle shrugged. "If there are other

commanders like this one in charge of area operations on other parts of the planet, then no. But possibly there is one queen…or king…out there, somewhere, directing it all."

Holmes pointed to the screen. "Rescue the prisoners and gather any additional intel you can to determine if they have a single leader."

Marcus nodded. "We will."

Cruz stepped closer to Santha. "We need to get this raptor commander's description to the drone operators. Have them on the lookout for her. If she is in charge in Sydney, then the prisoners can't be far from her."

"Elle?" Marcus said.

She lifted her tablet, swiping the screen. "On it."

Santha lifted her comp controller and changed the image to an aerial map of the city. She drew circles around four main raptor installations. "These are the four main places I've seen the commander most frequently."

Marcus nodded. "Good. I suggest we send in four recon teams. Each with two people only. Slip in, gather intel, confirm the prisoners are there and get out. Then we'll plan a rescue mission." He turned to his team. "Claudia and Shaw, you'll be one recon team."

Claudia straightened. "I want to go with Gabe—"

"It wasn't a suggestion." Marcus' tone hardened. "I'm with Gabe. Cruz and Santha will be the third team." He cursed. "We really need to fill the final squad spot. But for now, I'll ask Masters to head the fourth team with one of his guys from Squad Nine."

Cruz liked Squad Nine's leader a lot. No one was quite sure what Roth Masters' background was. Some said military, others said intelligence. Cruz could see the man as a soldier or a spy, but he didn't really care, as long as Roth was good at killing raptors and keeping his team alive.

Santha set the controller down. "When do we leave?"

"Tomorrow."

She started. "What? Those people are suffering God knows what—"

Marcus' eyes narrowed. "My team just spent the night in the field. Contrary to what everyone thinks, including them, they need sleep. And just a few hours ago you bled out, took a potent cocktail of stimulants, suffered a nano-med cascade *and* died. Those bugs might had fixed you up but you still need rest."

Cruz suppressed a wince. He'd been on the receiving end of that cold tone of Marcus' a time or two.

Marcus' gaze hit Cruz. "I assume I can trust you to make sure she gets some rest and doesn't go off half-cocked?"

When Santha stiffened more, Cruz was at least happy that the deep grief was gone from her face for the moment.

He grabbed her hand. "Come on, *mi reina*. Before you know it, you'll be covered in raptor blood and dodging poison again."

***

Santha felt like a wire strung too tight and ready to snap.

After eating lunch at a long table in the dining room, wedged between Cruz and a silent Gabe, she was feeling the need for some space. She hadn't even enjoyed the very fine meal of protein substitute and fresh—*fresh*—vegetables. It had reminded her of her favorite meal—Kareena's curry.

Santha wanted to be out there searching for the prisoners, not stuck in these tunnels. That's why she'd avoided the base so long—she liked being her own boss. Here, there were too many people who thought they could tell her what to do.

"Movie Night's on tonight. I think they're playing an old classic, something about robots taking over the world and killing humanity." Cruz snorted. "I'd take robots over aliens any day."

The thought of being stuck in an enclosed room full of people for a whole evening made a flutter of panic stir in Santha's belly. God, she'd clearly been alone too long.

She looked up and saw Cruz eyeing her like she was an open comp file.

"How about some fresh air?" he suggested.

It should annoy her that he could read her so clearly. She nodded. "Please."

He led through the maze of tunnels to a door. It had a sign marked with various warning messages.

He gestured her through, into a tiny tunnel only wide enough for one that sloped upward. At the top was another door closed with a round lock. Cruz reached around her and spun it.

They stepped out into the forest.

Sunlight filtered through the trees and Santha pulled in the fragrant air. It smelled...green. And fresh. So different to the city. Instantly, her muscles loosened.

Here the insects still chirped their songs and small animals scurried unseen in the bushes. They were going about their daily lives, mostly unaffected by the alien invasion.

If only humanity had been so lucky.

"You find it hard to be around so many people?"

God, that accent. His voice was like music in the darkness. "I've been alone for a year, Cruz. I've gotten...comfortable with my own company."

"I understand. I hated the base the first few months I was here. Marcus and I were over in Sydney for military maneuvers when the attack happened."

"You're from the United States, right?"

He nodded. "New Mexico. My father was Mexican and my mother American. And I have a sister."

"Do you know if they're still alive?"

"I've no idea." He stared at the trees. "I can only hope."

There was pain there, buried deep.

He glanced at her. "Although I do have a few family members I wouldn't mind having met with a messy death at the hands of the raptors."

She sucked in a breath. "What?"

Cruz rubbed the back of his neck. "Forget I said anything."

"Too late for that now, soldier." Santha found a fallen log and sat down. She wanted to know this man's secrets. "Tell me."

He stuck his hands on his hips, eyeing the grass. "My father...he escaped his family in Mexico. They ran a drug cartel."

She blinked. "He must have been tough to escape from that."

"Yeah. I was only a kid but he packed us up and ran. Although they tried a few times to kill him. Once they realized he wasn't heading off to sell their secrets or start his own rival cartel, they left him alone."

There was more to the story. She heard it in the dark edge to his words. "But?"

He released a long breath. "We'd moved to the U.S., but a cousin searched me out when I was finishing high school. I was going through a phase, not getting along with my dad. I was young, angry and keen to prove myself."

"They sucked you in."

"Yeah. I spent two years working for my uncle. I thought I was so tough." Brown eyes met hers and bored into her. "I did some terrible things. Unforgivable things."

She couldn't picture Cruz doing anything except what was right. "I heard Mexico got hit pretty hard in the invasion."

"Yeah." He was lost in his memories. "It would be a favor to the world if my uncle and cousin didn't make it."

"How did you get out?"

"The job had lost its shine a long time before I found the courage to leave. It wasn't fun, exciting or edgy anymore. I was an enforcer...I killed people." He shook his head. "Most of them were scum, but some weren't. I have to live with that. At the time, I felt like my soul was disappearing, little piece by little piece."

She knew that feeling. Felt it every day when she remembered Kareena, when she went out to fight the raptors.

"But there was one thing that finally made me snap. My cousin, Manuel...he'd always had a thing for young girls. They flocked to him and he joked how once they'd tasted his pleasures, they never wanted to leave. That he made them feel special." Cruz closed his eyes. "I should have known something was wrong. He never let anyone back to his cottage on my uncle's property. But one day, I needed to talk to him and he wasn't answering his phone." A grimace of disgust crossed Cruz's face. "He...had a torture chamber. None of those girls had left him, because he'd tied them up, was raping them, cutting them, torturing them."

Santha hissed in a breath.

"I never sunk as low as rape," Cruz said. "Or to fucking hurt kids, or cut a woman open..." He closed his eyes for a second. "Most of those girls died, but I made sure Manuel wouldn't hurt any more little girls and I went home."

"Your parents?"

"Welcomed me home. Told me they loved me." There was a sad smile on his face. "I had a hard time adjusting and knew if I didn't try and make amends, I'd probably end up an addict myself. I joined the United Coalition Marines instead."

"And here you are."

"Yeah, after a lot of blood, sweat and tears—" he stepped closer to her "—here I am." He reached out and fiddled with her hair, his fingers brushing against her ear. "So, you were SWAT?"

His touch had warmth flooding her and her pulse tripped. "Yes. I always knew that was what I wanted to do." She wrinkled her nose. "I like guns."

"Music to my ears, *querida.*"

She smiled. "I got a criminology degree, became a police officer and as soon as I was eligible, took the SWAT test."

"SWAT's not for the faint of heart."

"Nope. But I loved it. Had a great team." Her heart clenched. "They were killed in the invasion. I was on leave that day and they were annihilated in the fighting."

"I'm sorry."

"I was glad that at least I was with Kareena. But then a week later…"

"Tell me about her?"

"She was the sunshine. That's what my father used to call her. Our parents had us late in life and after they passed away, it was just the two of us. She laughed a lot and loved helping people. She was a nurse." Santha caught Cruz's gaze. It was nice to remember the good times. "And she was a great cook. Made the best chicken curry in the world. It was packed full of spices—turmeric, ginger, cumin. And she'd always make homemade chapattis, an Indian flatbread." Santha released a long breath. "God, I miss her cooking."

He smiled. "I understand. I still miss my dad's tamales." Cruz's fingers were back at her ear, tracing the shell.

All thoughts of her sister flew out of Santha's head. She gripped his wrist. "Cruz, this is crazy. We barely know each other. We have other things to focus on…this just gets in the way."

His hand settled on her neck, his thumb brushing against her racing pulse. "We do know each other. We know the stuff that counts. I know you're stubborn, intelligent, can handle a crossbow, and so courageous it scares the hell out of me."

She frowned. "That doesn't sound very attractive."

He nudged her closer to him. "I'm a soldier, *mi reina*. Believe me, watching you handle a crossbow is goddamned foreplay."

She pressed her palms to his chest and laughed. God, it felt good. And so did he. He was hard and smelled good. The tattoo wrapped around his bicep drew her gaze. Drawn to it, she traced a finger over the design. "You're all those things as well. I could probably throw *arrogant* and *alpha male* in there, too."

He tipped her chin up and her heart started

beating faster. She was helpless to resist this man.

"Then we're made for each other," he murmured.

Santha licked her lips, saw his eyes zero in on the move. "I got the impression you have plenty of willing playmates here at base."

"I don't want any of them. I want you." He leaned down and nipped her lip. "Only you, *mi reina.*"

Dammit, why shouldn't she just leap before looking? The world had gone to hell, things weren't like they were before, where she'd date a nice guy and then take him to her bed. Now you took what you wanted and grabbed it with both hands, because you never knew when it might be yanked from your grasp.

The thought of a few scorching, sweaty hours with Cruz moving thickly between her legs made Santha feel hot and electric. For a few hours, she could forget and just focus on pleasure.

"Cruz, let's—"

Something vibrated in Cruz's pocket. He cursed under his breath. "My communicator." He yanked it out and checked the screen. Instantly, the slumberous, heated look in his eyes vanished. "One of the drones has found something."

Santha straightened, and gave her head a small shake. Moving from thinking about sex to the mission jarred her. "What? What was it?"

His head snapped up. "They didn't say. But they want us in Ops."

"Then let's go."

Together, they hurried back into the base. At a

half jog, they made it to the Operations Area and into the Hive.

Marcus and Elle were there with General Holmes.

"What is it?" Santha demanded.

Marcus nodded at a curvy, redheaded woman in a blue uniform at the desk nearby. "Lia here, thinks she's found something."

The redhead's short, feathered hair accented a long, slim neck and a face dominated by large almond-shaped eyes. "I spotted a group of raptors bringing supplies into one of the bases that had been marked as a potential location for the prisoners."

"Supplies?" Cruz frowned, crossing his arms over his chest. "That isn't unusual."

"No." Lia turned. "But one of them dropped a box and the contents spilled out." She tapped at her comp and an image flashed on the huge screen on the wall.

It showed vegetables spilled out on the pavement.

"I don't get it," Marcus said. "Potatoes and spinach, so what?"

But Santha's pulse tripped. "Raptors are carnivorous. They don't eat plants."

"You think this is to feed the prisoners?" Cruz said.

"It's a possibility," Lia replied. "I flagged it as a potential item of interest. Then someone special turned up a few minutes later."

The image changed and this time Santha felt a

punch of heat to her gut.

It was the commander.

"We need to get to this location and check it out," she said. "I don't care about resting. I'm going. *Now*."

Holmes held up a hand. "Calm down, Santha. I've already given the order for the recon mission supplies to be readied for the four recon teams." His gaze moved between her and Cruz. "Go."

Chapter Seven

Cruz led Santha into the hangar bay.

They were prepped and ready to head out. Beside him, Santha was fiddling with the armor he'd found for her. It was all-black, and the lightest he could find. The carbon fiber panels slicked over her long, lean body.

"You okay?"

She gave a distracted nod. "I'm not used to wearing stuff like this."

"That 'stuff' can stop raptor claws, or one of their projectiles. You're more likely to survive in it."

She touched the laser pistols holstered at her hips and the frag grenades lined up along her belt. "I'm just not used to being this...decked out."

"Advantage of being at the base. We have good supplies."

She nodded. "Still, I feel naked without my crossbow."

"Well..." he moved to the wall and grabbed what he'd stashed there earlier. He handed it to her.

Her mouth dropped open as she took her matte-black crossbow. "Where did you get this?"

"I asked Claudia to bring it with us when we evaced from your apartment. It was a little damaged, but I did some work to it." He'd spent some of those endless hours she'd been unconscious in the infirmary slaving over it.

She stroked the crossbow like a lover and Cruz's mouth went dry. When she looked up, warmth glowed in her green eyes. "Thank you." She walked to him, went up on her toes and kissed him.

The kiss was over too fast. He wanted to grab her and drag her away somewhere private. *Later*, he promised himself.

Santha secured the crossbow on her back. "So, are we taking a Hawk into the city?"

"Nope. We need a bit more stealth than that." He reached up and brushed the lobe of her ear. "I have something else for you." He slipped a tiny earpiece into her ear. "Elle, you there?"

"Read you loud and clear, Cruz," Elle's voice came through their earpieces.

"Santha's online too."

"Hey, Santha."

Santha touched her ear. "Elle."

"You need anything—intel, escape routes, raptor numbers—just ask, okay?"

Santha blinked. Cruz could see it was another thing she was adjusting to. An uncomfortable feeling slithered through him. What if she couldn't get used to all the people, the structure and the other stuff that came with being at base?

What if after this mission, she didn't want to stay here?

"All right, soldier." She held her palms up. "Let's go spy on some raptors."

He nodded, shaking off his thoughts. He couldn't afford to think about it right now. He needed a clear head and laser-sharp focus.

"So, if Hawks are out, how are we getting into the city?" she asked.

He waved her toward a door to the next hangar bay. As they stepped inside the dark space, lights clicked on automatically.

"This is our ride."

Santha gasped. "I've never seen anything like it."

"It's called a Darkswift. We use them for covert infiltration." He watched her circle the sleek, black craft barely big enough to fit two people. "It's shaped like a glider, seats two people lying down side by side on their stomachs. There are dual controls—" he pointed to the tinted, low-profile canopy "—and it has a small, silent, thermonuclear engine."

She looked up and smiled. "I *cannot* wait to try it out. Let's go."

Cruz opened the canopy. "Climb aboard."

She stepped in and lay flat on her stomach in the molded space. "Can I fly it?" Excitement vibrated in her voice.

"No."

She frowned at him over her shoulder. "Why not?"

"You have to be trained."

She snorted. "That's a bullshit excuse. You're just being a man...won't let a woman drive."

Cruz arched a brow. "Yes, I want to drive. I'd

prefer we didn't end up crashing into the side of a building. And in case you hadn't noticed, I am a man."

Something flashed in her eyes. "Oh, I noticed."

He let his gaze drift down her body, lingering on her shapely ass. Man, he really didn't need a hard-on in his armor. Sucking in a breath, he lay down on the other side of the Darkswift's cockpit.

They were only inches apart. He thumbed a control and the smoky-black canopy closed.

"How come I haven't seen any of these babies flying around?"

"They have illusion systems and because they're small and silent, they're easy to hide. And we usually only use them at night. They're practically invisible."

"Cool."

He smiled at her. "Ready to launch?"

"Ready."

"Elle, we are a go for launch."

"Okay, Cruz," Elle said. "Initiating launch now. Good luck."

Cruz adjusted the controls. A neon-green, heads-up display flared to life in front of him and harnesses snapped closed over their bodies. "There's a launch mechanism in the floor beneath us. It'll catapult us into the air."

"How do we launch to come back?"

"The engine can get us airborne, but not as high as we'd like for maximum stealth."

Elle counted down steadily in their ears. Ahead, the launch bay doors retracted, revealing a strip of early-evening sky. Below, the valley was a mass of shadows.

"Hold on," he warned.

Santha gripped the handholds built into the console. A second later, the catapult mechanism released and sent the Darkswift shooting out of the hangar.

As they soared into the air, Santha laughed.

Cruz tapped the controls, his right hand gently moving the control stick. He monitored the display as the computer their checked altitude and adjusted the stabilizers.

Then he turned his head and was caught by the sight of unfettered joy on her face. It made his gut cramp. He suspected she'd had little to laugh about since the invasion.

Finally, their ascent leveled out, and the engine kicked in, sending them gliding silently toward the city.

"I have to get myself one of these," Santha said. "Are you sure I can't have a turn flying it?"

"I'm sure."

A pause. "Maybe I could bribe you with something?"

The slight, seductive drawl in her voice made him go hard. *Dammit.* "You probably could."

"Hmm, I just have to work out what I have that you want."

He caught her gaze. "I want everything you have. All of it."

Her smile evaporated and she just stared at him. "I'm not that special."

"We covered this already. Brave, helps others and never gives up."

She snorted. "I'm not a saint, Cruz."

"I know. I don't want a saint. Believe me, once I get you in bed, or against a wall, I want the opposite of saintly."

A faint blush stained her cheeks. "When we get back from this recon mission, then we'll see."

Oh, yeah, they would. "Now, stop distracting me. A hard-on in armor is really uncomfortable."

As she laughed again, he turned his attention to the controls. They soared in over the outskirts of the city. Elle updated him on raptor troop movements on the ground, but thankfully, the air space was free.

"We'll land in a strip of parkland by the harbor and then go in on foot," he said. "It's about two kilometers to the raptor installation. There's a row of old shops and restaurants next door, we'll use the roof as a vantage point."

Santha nodded. "Got it."

As the computer guided them into the landing area, Cruz felt that familiar tingle he got in his blood just before his boots hit dirt on a mission. A clarity, an intense focus that couldn't be matched by anything else.

"Get ready for landing."

Their speed dropped off and eventually the engine cut out. Cruz glided them in and they scooted across the grass, the reverse thrusters making them stop before they neared the water.

Touch down.

***

"Hell of a ride, soldier," Santha said.

"I'm sure I could say something inappropriate to that comment, *querida*."

She grinned. The man really was too sexy for his own good. And that accent...she thought hearing it more would make her immune to it.

Nope. "I bet you could." She touched the control for the canopy and it slid open. "But we have a mission."

They both climbed out of the Darkswift. Santha checked her crossbow before sliding it over her shoulder. Across the glider, Cruz did the same with his carbine.

He strode around to join her. "You need to activate your combat helmet." He touched the side of her neck, his fingers brushing over skin until he found a button at the neck of her armor. The helmet extended from her armor, sliding over her head.

"Neat," she said.

"It's made of a thin, extremely strong thermoplastic." He activated his own. "Now, I suggest you take the lead."

"What?"

"You know this city better than anyone. I'd be crazy not to use your expertise."

She hitched her crossbow up and nodded. God, the man just kept making her like him more.

After a quick glance at the comp screen attached

to her wrist to check the map Elle had uploaded for them, she headed off. "We'll stick to the buildings along the water's edge and use them for cover."

He tapped the side of his helmet. "There's a button here to activate your night-vision lens." A small eyepiece slipped over his right eye.

She flicked hers on. The night showed up in shades of green. They fell into a quick pace, Cruz following closely behind her, a warm, intense presence. She moved quickly and quietly, sticking to the shadows. She fell into her usual way of moving to stay invisible.

That was the key to this mission, being invisible. In and out. They'd get their intel, confirm the prisoners were either at this raptor installation or not, and then get out.

So why did she have a huge gnawing sensation in her gut that a big pile of crap was headed their way?

Santha suddenly halted and pushed her back against the wall. Cruz followed suit and gripped his carbine. She tilted her head, listening. She was positive she'd heard something.

"Cruz?" Elle's voice in their ears. "There's a small raptor patrol about two hundred meters from your location. They just appeared on the map, Must have come out of the sewers or some other hidey-hole."

Cruz just tapped his earpiece to acknowledge the information and remained silent.

They waited for several minutes before Santha relaxed and nodded. The raptors had moved on.

"You move like the wind," Cruz murmured.

The compliment warmed her. They moved past apartment buildings, large houses, and boutique stores. In the street, cars were piled on top of each other, some just burned out shells.

She wanted to believe a rex had done the damage, the giant creature tearing through what had once been an affluent suburb. But she knew a good portion of the destruction had been caused by humans. In the initial invasion, many people had panicked and gone into hiding or escaped the city. Others had looted and rioted, and in the days that followed, most had given in to the incredible terror.

Cruz and Santha kept moving. They reached a park area by the harbor. The grass was lush and green from the recent rain and rose to past her knees. They waded in and Santha was glad it was nighttime. All the snakes should be holed up somewhere else.

She stopped under a tree and leaned in close to Cruz. "Just around the next bend, we'll be able to see the raptor base." She tapped her mini-comp. "We only have to cover another two hundred meters and we'll be at our vantage point."

Cruz nodded.

They moved on, and soon, the trees and plants of the park grew closer together into a dense bush. Santha pushed her way through it, branches slapping at her and grass seed sticking to her boots.

A flash of movement through the long grass caught her eye.

She stopped. For a second, she thought she'd imagined it. She wasn't used to the night vision and the way it changed her surroundings.

A sound. A large body moving through the bush.

Another sound. A strange animal noise. She frowned. It didn't sound like anything she'd ever heard before.

"Santha?"

"Shh." She stayed still. The sound came again, a cross between a gurgle and a click. A chill swept over her.

"What was that?" Cruz said.

"Cruz and Santha," Elle's steady voice came over the line. "I'm picking up a heat signature near you guys. It isn't a rex but it looks larger than a raptor. The growth is too thick and it's too dark for a visual."

"Roger that, Elle," Cruz responded with a quiet murmur.

Santha turned, trying to find the animal. Maybe it was some escaped pet? A horse? A large dog?

Yeah, and maybe the raptors were really here to make friends. She pulled her crossbow out. "Let's keep moving. Slowly."

They covered more ground and nothing appeared or charged them. But the sensation of being watched didn't dissipate.

She felt a groove in the dirt beneath her feet. She stopped and crouched. Cruz flicked on the light on his carbine and aimed it down.

A large footprint, with three clawed toes, was perfectly delineated in the damp ground where the long grass lay broken and flattened.

Cruz made a sound in his throat. "That is no dog."

No. It was larger than a dog print, much, much larger and with much sharper claws.

"Pick up speed." She wanted to get them out of this grass. It hampered their movements and vision.

The strange sound came again. From the left.

They moved into a jog.

The sound again. On the right.

That shiver hit Santha again. "It's hunting us."

"Fucker can show himself and see how he likes my carbine," Cruz muttered. His voice was in no way quiet.

"Shh! Don't antagonize it."

"We don't even know what *it* is."

Suddenly a large, dark body burst from the undergrowth and slammed into Cruz. They smashed into the ground.

There was enough moonlight for her to make out the large, feathered creature trying to slash at Cruz's abdomen with the huge sickle-shaped claw on its hind foot.

Santha's brain cleared of everything except one thought. *Kill it. Stop it hurting Cruz.*

She fired a bolt into its side.

The bolt glanced off and fell to the ground.

Next she aimed for its head.

This time the bolt hit, but she could tell it hadn't penetrated far enough to do much damage.

The creature whipped its head around and bared

its razor-sharp teeth. God, the damn thing was fast, and those claws did not look like they were for show.

Santha walked closer, saw Cruz struggling beneath the creature.

Its red gaze flicked up and it watched Santha approach. It was probably wondering why she wasn't running and screaming. It had hunted humans before, she was certain of it. It had taken Cruz out first—what it perceived as the biggest threat—and, based on the deep scratches on Cruz's armor, it clearly knew where to slash to kill a human.

Thank God Cruz was wearing body armor.

Santha aimed her next bolt at the sliver of softer underbelly she could see.

The alien gave an almost human scream and reared back. Santha rushed to Cruz's side.

He was already getting up. Despite the grooves in his armor, there was no blood.

He lifted his carbine and started firing at the creature. Santha followed suit.

The alien leaped into the bush and both of them followed. She had no idea if this creature could communicate with the other raptors, or if it was more like a hunting dog following simple orders.

But Santha didn't want to take any chances. And she'd seen a naked intelligence in the creature's eyes. She didn't think it was a mindless hunting dog like the canids.

"Shit, where is it?" Cruz cursed.

She crouched. "Prints."

She tracked it, following its prints until they just...disappeared.

"What the hell?" she muttered.

Cruz stiffened. "Santha—"

A huge weight dropped from the tree above and knocked into Santha. She felt the sting of claws at her neck and heard that horrible gurgling click again.

As she slammed into the ground, she lost her grip on the crossbow. She felt the animal clawing at her belly. Tearing at her armor.

Chapter Eight

Cruz's carbine sounded hellishly loud. Santha slid her hand into her belt and yanked out the combat knife Cruz had given her.

She reached up and stabbed the creature in its belly.

It let out a scream, its clawing becoming more frenzied.

Dammit, why wouldn't it die? For the first time in a long time, Santha felt a fierce need to survive. She yanked the knife out and sank it into the alien's neck.

Its mouth opened, its terrible teeth only inches from her face.

She felt hot blood splash over her. The alien slumped forward, knocking the wind out of her.

"Santha!" Cruz was there, hefting the creature off her. He yanked her to her feet. "Is any of the blood yours? Where are you hurt?"

"Not mine." She tried to catch her breath and calm her racing heart.

He was patting her down, a savage look in his brown eyes.

Damn, there was that warm glow again. The man was turning her to mush. She cupped his cheeks. "Cruz. I'm okay."

Finally his gaze met hers, the primal intensity receding. "You're sure?

"Positive." She leaned up and kissed him.

When she pulled back, a different kind of heat was warming her. If the fire glowing in his eyes was anything to go by, he felt the same.

His hand wrapped around her braid. "When we get back to base…"

She licked her lips. "Yes?"

He jerked her forward. "I'm fucking you. Hard."

"Not if I fuck you first." She turned away to snatch up her crossbow and let her cheeks cool. The adrenaline rush and fear thundering in her blood turned to pure lust in a flash.

When she turned back, Cruz was watching her, those dark eyes burning hot. She was sure a few sweaty sessions between them would burn out this heat arcing between them.

He heaved in a few breaths. "You're hell on my concentration." He pulled a tiny camera off his belt. "We need to snap a few pics of this…thing. The geek squad'll want to take a look."

He kicked the alien over, uncovering those vicious claws. God, they were lucky it hadn't shredded them into ribbons.

After he finished the photos, he touched his earpiece. "Elle, you got a drone in range so I can send you some images?"

"Yes. Are you two okay? I couldn't see what you were fighting."

"We're fine. I'm uploading images of the

creature. Some unknown kind of alien. And it's not nice and fluffy."

"They're coming through now." Elle's quick intake of breath came through loud over the line. "You're lucky to be alive! We'll start analyzing it. Be careful."

Cruz glanced at Santha. "Let's get out of this long grass. I don't want to run into any more of these."

Santha took the lead again and soon they left the park and were back amongst the buildings. A wind had picked up, blowing wisps of her hair around her face. At least it was drying the blood splattered all over her.

"There." She pointed to a row of what had once been shops. "See the roof? It's flat and there are air-conditioning units we can use for cover. On the other side of that row of buildings is the school the raptors have taken over as their base."

Cruz eyed the roof. "Not too high to climb. There's a dumpster at the end we can use to get up."

They worked together. She climbed up onto the dumpster and he followed with one lithe jump and a flex of his muscled arm. From there, he kneeled and cupped his hands together. She pressed her boot to his hands and with an easy lift, she flew up and gripped the edge of the roof. She pulled herself over and crouched. A second later, Cruz pulled himself over the ledge.

Bent over, they hurried across the roof to one of the large, industrial air-conditioning units. They pressed their backs to the metal, then peered around.

Below, the schoolyard was filled with raptors.

Out of habit, Santha ducked a little lower. The aliens had lights set up, illuminating the entire yard. Some raptors were clearly on guard, holding weapons. Others were shifting supplies into the main building. A side door was propped open.

"Good vantage point." Cruz settled down on the ground next to her, his sharp gaze assessing their enemies. "Bastards look fucking cozy, don't they?"

"We'll find a way to get rid of them," she murmured.

A muscle ticked in his jaw but he nodded.

Santha was shocked at her words. She'd only ever cared about revenge. When had she started caring about driving these invading bastards away?

Below, the raptors stirred, the guards coming to attention.

A throaty growl of an engine echoed through the streets.

"Someone's coming." Santha arched her neck to get a better look.

One of the squat raptor transports pulled into view, its lights spearing into the night. It was followed by two vans, and Santha scowled. Now it appeared the raptors were using human vehicles, too.

The raptor soldiers in the yard formed two rough lines. A tall figure got out of the lead vehicle.

Santha bit her lip hard enough to sting. The commander.

Quickly, Santha pressed down onto her belly and scuttled closer to the edge of the roof for a better view.

"Santha!" Cruz bit out on a savage whisper.

Crouched by the ledge, she carefully peered over. A second later, Cruz's big body moved in beside hers.

She kept her gaze glued to the commander. Memories hit like bullets: Kareena's screams as a raptor kicked her, her blood soaking onto the ground, the commander watching on impassively.

Santha had fought to move, but her body hadn't obeyed. She'd screamed, but it'd been soundless.

She remembered the grunts and strange guttural language of the raptors. Then that last glimpse of her sister as they'd dragged Kareena's lifeless body away.

With a blink, Santha snapped back to the present. She heard the commander issue some throaty commands to the raptors below before she swept up the front steps and into the building.

Santha's hand curled into a fist. "We need to get closer."

"No," Cruz said through gritted teeth. "Recon only."

"I'm not going to engage—"

He snorted. "Yeah, right. Waltz right into the middle of their base, but not engage."

"We need proof that the prisoners are being held inside. We can't get it from here."

"We need to be patient. Not a word in your vocab, I know. But we both know the reason you want to go in there isn't because you're after intel."

Santha worked to keep her face composed. "I care about finding those prisoners—"

His face was set. "I never said you didn't. But you've been living and breathing revenge for a year. I know you want that commander dead."

She didn't respond. She didn't like that she was so damn transparent. Dammit, she could balance her need to find the prisoners with the driving desire to see the commander dead.

Elle's voice came through the earpiece. "Cruz, General Holmes would like an update."

"Roger that, Elle." Cruz turned to the side to block the wind from his earpiece.

An idea gripped Santha and her muscles tensed. She glanced down at the side door propped open, then at the raptors now milling near the vehicles. Cruz was still talking quietly.

He'd kill her for this.

Santha closed her eyes for a second and forced herself to think of Kareena. Her smile, her witty sense of humor, her blood splattered on the ground.

Santha crawled backward, moving with all the stealth her training had drilled into her and a year of living on the edge had honed sharp.

With one final guilt-soaked glance at Cruz's broad back, she slipped over the edge of the roof.

**

"Got it, Elle. We'll report in soon."

"Stay safe, Cruz," Elle replied.

Cruz turned to update Santha and realized she was no longer beside him. His gut clenched and he scanned the rooftop.

But he already knew.

Staying low, he peered over the ledge...

In time to see her slipping unseen into the open doorway into the raptor base.

"Fucking hell!" His hands curled into fists, his muscles straining. He should have known she'd try a stunt like this.

He should call it in...but he knew Holmes would forbid him following her. And Elle would see the instant Cruz moved inside. He hesitated for half a second, then touched his earpiece, deactivating his comms.

Dammit to hell, when he caught up with Santha, he was going to tie her up. Preferably to his bed.

In a crouch, he moved along the length of the building and slipped over the edge right at the farthest point from the raptors.

Seconds later, he was moving across the open area toward the door, using anything he could for cover.

He paused about four meters from the door, hidden behind a stack of boxes. He heard the scrape of a boot and ducked down. The noisy breathing of the passing raptor guard made Cruz tense. He slipped his gladius combat knife out, tensed, ready to kill if he had to.

He couldn't attract any other raptor attention. Not just to protect himself but to protect Santha. If the raptors saw him, they'd go into lockdown and she'd be stuck inside.

Or worse, captured.

Another scrape of a boot.

And then the guard moved on.

Cruz relaxed a fraction, but his adrenaline was up and he'd need it to get inside and yank Santha out of there.

After checking the raptors were focused elsewhere, he raced out from behind cover and through the door.

Inside was an empty corridor. He brought his carbine up and moved forward.

He came to the first doorway and checked the room. A classroom. Tables and chairs sitting neatly in rows. But empty.

He kept moving. *Where the hell are you, Santha?*

The next two rooms were empty of people or aliens but filled with supplies and items of interest the raptors were stockpiling.

As Cruz moved farther down the hall, he thought he heard the distant murmur of voices but he couldn't quite make out the sounds.

At the next doorway, he saw a living area of sorts. The raptors had pushed together some chairs and tables. Some sort of animal had become a meal and the remnants of raw meat and picked bones sat on a table. Cruz grimaced and was about to turn when he caught a flicker of movement out the corner of his eye. He swung his carbine around, finger on the trigger.

Santha appeared out of the shadows, arms raised.

Cruz cursed and lowered his weapon. "What the fuck do you think you're doing?"

"Seeing if the prisoners are here. Seeing what the commander is doing here."

He shook his head. "This is reckless, Santha. No plan, no warning. You'll get us killed."

"You didn't have to come. And I've survived this long doing things exactly like this."

"Dumb luck."

"Screw you—"

He gripped the nape of her neck. "I fucking care, Santha. Get used to it."

A shiver wracked her and the fire leaked out of her eyes. "I know. I'm sorry."

"Sorry isn't going to cut it. You'll have to do much better than that to make it up to me when we get back to base."

Her eyes narrowed. "Are you blackmailing me into giving you sex?"

"I didn't say anything about sex."

She snorted. "No, you just implied heavily."

"I didn't imply a damn thing," he bit out. "When we have sex, it'll be because we both want it. Got it?"

She inclined her head.

He sucked in a deep breath. "Any sign of the prisoners?"

Her face screwed up. "No. But I did find something weird." She waved him over to another doorway.

Inside were large, rounded...well, he wasn't sure what they were. They were about the size of single beds but had a dome-like cover made from a translucent orange substance. They were ribbed with what looked like...veins.

"I think this is where the raptors sleep," Santha whispered, moving closer to the nearest pod. "They're like a bed crossed with an egg." She reached out a hand.

"Don't touch it!"

She stopped just short of the organic, amber-like substance. Suddenly the dome cover moved, opening with a quiet hiss.

Santha stumbled backward. Cruz lifted his weapon.

The pod was empty.

They both studied it. There was a space inside that would fit a raptor.

Cruz lifted his camera and snapped a few images. "Come on. We're here now, so let's take a quick look around."

They moved through the corridors, finding more living quarters for the raptors, more supplies, empty classrooms.

No human prisoners.

He saw Santha's face becoming more and more grim.

"They have to be here," she said.

He glanced at his watch. "We can't stay much longer."

"We have to keep searching the building. The—"

Heavy footsteps sounded around the corner, farther down the hall.

Shit. Cruz glanced around. Not many places to hide. He gripped Santha's arm and urged her down the corridor.

More footsteps. Coming from the opposite direction. He stopped. Dammit, they were trapped between oncoming raptors.

He yanked out his knife and gestured for her to stay behind him.

Then he leaped around the corridor corner.

The raptor strolling toward them reared back, startled, and dropped his weapon. Cruz slammed into him.

The alien didn't go down. He was a big bastard. When his gaze landed on Cruz, the red in his eyes flared.

Cruz reversed his grip on the knife hilt and plunged the blade into the side of the alien's neck. Cruz worked the knife in, blocking the raptor's swinging fist with his other arm.

The raptor didn't even get a chance to make a noise. He died in an instant and Cruz rode his body to the ground.

"Come on!" she whispered frantically. "More are coming."

The drum of boots was like a metronome ticking down the time. Cruz grabbed the dead raptor under his armpits and dragged him down the hall. "We have to find somewhere to stash this guy."

"Ah...there's blood on the floor."

"Clean it up best you can. It's not like they're

keeping the place tidy." The floor was filthy.

She screwed up her nose but quickly used her boot to smear the blood into the other dirt stains.

"They're coming!" She glanced down the hall.

"Quick, there's a janitor's closet."

Together, they got the door open and with some awkward maneuvering, got the heavy body of the dead raptor into the closet. The space turned out to be more like a small room filled with shelves of cleaning products, brooms, mops and an industrial floor cleaner.

Santha had just eased the door closed when they heard the thud of running boots and the guttural sounds of raptors talking.

Cruz quietly lowered the body to the floor, all his attention focused on the threat outside. If they had to fight their way out, being trapped in this tiny room wouldn't be to their advantage.

But the sound of the raptors quickly faded away.

Santha's shoulders relaxed. "They're gone."

"But they were searching for someone. They know we're here. And once they realize they have a guard missing, they'll be back." Cruz studied their hiding place.

He dragged the raptor body back behind a shelf to keep it hidden from a cursory search.

Santha shoved her hands on her hips. "What should we do—?"

A low moan filled the room.

Cruz glanced at the raptor. It was still and silent.

Another strangled cry, low and pitiful.

"What the hell?" Santha whispered, hefting her crossbow.

He looked around and spotted a large ventilation grille. When the moaning started again, he realized the sound was filtering through there.

He pointed, and with a nod, Santha followed him over.

They crouched and peered through the slats of the vent.

Cruz's gut clenched and an explosive curse escaped his mouth.

Santha pressed a closed fist to her lips. "Oh, my God."

Chapter Nine

Santha's brain couldn't compute what she was seeing.

Through the narrow gaps in the vent, she could see several narrow beds lined against the wall in the dim room.

In each bed was a human...being experimented on.

Closest to her and Cruz, she saw a man hooked up to so many organic-like tubes he was barely visible. Blood ran out of some tubes, and other fluids of various colors were running into him. He was thrashing weakly and moaning.

The next bed held a woman with her chest cracked open and held apart by strange-looking bone claws. She was weeping.

Beside her was another woman, her pregnant stomach distended to an abnormally large size. She looked unconscious but her body was twitching spasmodically.

The row of beds continued, disappearing into the darkness. Holding who knew how many other people.

Bile rose in Santha's throat. They were lab rats. For whatever the hell the raptors were doing in here.

She swallowed, trying not to be sick. "We have to get them out."

She hadn't even realized she'd spoken until Cruz's big hands clasped hers, holding her in place. "We'll get them out. But we can't do it alone."

Something in his voice alerted her. A dark edge she'd never heard before. Staring up at his face, she saw a rage so black and lethal it scared her.

"It reminds you of your cousin," she said.

A muscle ticked in Cruz's jaw and he gave one curt nod.

"I don't want to leave them here one minute more," Santha whispered.

His hands tightened on hers. "Neither do I. But we need manpower and a medical team to help them."

Everything he said was true, but it tore at her. To leave anyone like this...she let out a long, unsteady breath. "We get back to base, get reinforcements and make a plan—" she stared into his dark eyes "—then we come back here and get them out."

"You got it, *mi reina*." He pressed a hand to the grate, his muscles flexing. "We'll be back."

Santha was about to pull back when she heard a small cry just on the other side of the grille. Startled, she pulled back, then slowly leaned forward again.

A green eye stared back at her.

Santha gasped. It was a girl. About ten years old.

She wore a filthy, tattered nightgown and her face was streaked with dirt. Half her head had been shaved, the other half was covered in a cloud of tangled dark hair.

Santha's heart was a heavy pound in her chest. The girl reminded her of a young Kareena with her dark hair and green eyes.

"Sweetheart, are you okay?" Santha whispered.

"What the hell?" Cruz crouched down. When he saw the girl, he pressed a fist to the wall and looked like he wanted to knock the bricks down.

The girl simply blinked at Santha, her expression vacant.

She had to be in shock. Other than the missing hair and the filth covering her, she looked fine.

"We're going to get you out of there." Santha couldn't save her sister but she sure as hell could save this little girl. Santha tested the strength of the grille over the vent. If she could just get it off—

Again, Cruz grabbed her hand. "Santha—"

"I'm not leaving her!" A furious whisper.

"We can't get out of here if she's with us."

"She looks just like Kareena did as a girl." Santha bit her lip. "I can't leave her."

He sighed and pressed a palm to the wall, his head dropping. "We could get killed or captured, we could get her killed trying to escape. And we wouldn't be able to come back for the others. Besides, she might need medical attention we can't give her."

"She looks fine, Cruz." Santha yanked at the grate again. She needed something to get the screws off. "Now help me, dammit."

From somewhere in the lab, there was the sound of a door opening and raptor voices.

The girl whimpered, her eyes going large.

"I'm getting you out." Santha yanked at the items on her belt. There had to be something that would work.

Then the girl turned. Santha's heart sank to her knees, a sob catching in her chest.

The shaved side of her head was covered in small round circles. Each one was a hole drilled into her skull. Some had tiny wires protruding from them.

Santha's arms dropped to her sides and she closed her eyes. They couldn't risk taking her outside, where God knew what could get into her open wounds.

Cruz's arm wrapped around Santha's shoulders. "We'll come back for her. We won't leave her."

The raptor voices were getting louder. With one more frightened look at them, the girl darted away.

"We have to go." Cruz pulled Santha away from the vent.

At the door to the storage room, he cupped her shoulders. "I need you back in the game so we can get out of here."

She nodded dully, but images of that raptor lab remained in her vision, burned into her brain.

"Santha." He shook her a little. "Focus."

"Okay, goddammit, I'm focused." She drew in a

big breath. "We get out. Then we come back."

He nodded. "I promise."

"Okay."

Santha focused on getting out of the raptor base. She couldn't let her thoughts stray to what she'd seen, to that little girl.

They moved rapidly through the halls. Three times, they had to dart into side rooms to hide as raptor troops passed by.

Don't think about the lab.

They managed to sneak out of the building without being seen. They sprinted out of the schoolyard and behind a neighboring building that used to be a restaurant.

Don't think about the lab.

Moving into a jog, they headed back toward the Darkswift. Ruthlessly, Santha choked off thoughts of that little girl and how she'd been violated.

"Let's skirt the park," Cruz murmured. "I don't want to run into another one of those feathered monsters."

Santha nodded.

It took a little longer, but they went around the long grass. She forced herself to stay alert for any signs of raptors or other alien creatures. But all she could hear were the echoes of those pained human moans.

They reached the Darkswift. Santha strapped in and Cruz started the engine. The canopy clicked into place.

"Elle, we're preparing for takeoff."

"Cruz! Where have you been? Marcus and

Holmes have been driving everyone crazy."

"We…ran into a little trouble. We can confirm the human prisoners are at the location."

Elle hissed in a breath. "Okay. Good. The other recon teams didn't find anything."

The Darkswift rose into the air. Santha watched the ground below get smaller and smaller, then they shot forward. Moments later they were heading west.

Away from the raptor base.

Away from the humans who needed their help.

Santha leaned forward until her forehead rested on the console. A helpless churn of anger and sorrow burned through her.

For the first time ever, she was glad Kareena had died. She would never, ever have wanted her sister to end up like that little girl.

Opening her eyes, Santha turned her head to look at the man beside her. The heads-up display cast a green glow over his hard features.

And for the first time in an eternity, she was glad she wasn't alone.

***

"You're got to be fucking kidding me." The words exploded out of Marcus.

Holmes stood nearby, face grim.

Cruz had just finished debriefing them on their recon mission and the raptors' experimentation.

He'd uploaded the images he'd taken to the comp and they flashed up on the screen. Beside him, he felt Santha tense.

The face of the little girl was like that of a ghost in the murky light of the lab. But it was enough to see the horrors going on behind her and the trauma reflected in the girl's blank green eyes.

Marcus cursed some more and Gabe, Shaw and Claudia joined him. Tears shimmered in Elle's eyes and Holmes looked ready to hit someone.

"Christ," Roth muttered. Squad Nine's leader had his arms crossed over his broad chest and his gaze glued to the screen.

Looking at that girl's face took Cruz back to another time, when he'd seen a room full of horrors and children being hurt. Ragged emotions were a storm in his gut.

But it was Santha he was most worried about.

She'd barely said a word on the way back to base, not even as they'd landed the Darkswift. Her face was scarily blank, but he felt the tension pouring off her. Something dark and ugly was brewing inside her, feeding on her thirst for revenge.

He was afraid of just what she'd risk to see it through.

Cruz half listened as the others scrolled through the images and stopped to discuss the alien they wrestled with in the park.

"It looks like a velociraptor." Elle tapping at the comp controls.

More images appeared, showing a dinosaur skeleton of an animal that looked similar to what had attacked them.

"Here's a rendering of what they thought the velociraptor would have looked like."

Cruz straightened. "Shit. That's eerily similar." A feathered dinosaur with huge claws on its back feet. The raptor version was a little larger.

"How many more of these are there?" Holmes asked.

"Impossible to know," Elle said.

"What will we call it?" This from Shaw.

"A velox," Elle said. "Velociraptor was named from the Latin word velox, meaning swift or rapid."

"Well, it was damn fast," Santha said. "Velox works."

Damn, Cruz really didn't like the calm face she was putting on.

"All right," Holmes said. "We'll plan a rescue mission. But I want an airtight plan. Whatever the raptors are doing, they aren't going to want to lose their test subjects. We have to have every move planned out, with a plan B and plan C mapped out as well, in case things go bad."

"We'll need two squads to go in," Marcus said.

"As well as a medical team," Elle added.

"We'll need the best." Marcus stared at the screen, his muscled arms crossed. "Hell Squad and Squad Nine."

"Hell, yeah," Roth said.

"Nine have been out working on base defenses," Holmes said. "And Steele, your team and Roth have been out on recon. I need everyone to get some rest, then in the morning we'll start planning."

Santha was already moving, but Cruz grabbed

her. She struggled in his hold. "No more resting or waiting. We need to get them out."

"We will," Cruz whispered in her ear.

"We'll get them out," Holmes reiterated. "But we won't go in half-cocked and risk our best fighters."

Santha twisted and Cruz had to tighten his grip to keep hold of her. "They're opening them up, drilling into their heads—"

"I know." Something flashed in Holmes' eyes. "I know. But you risked yourself and Cruz's life today. I don't have that luxury. I have to think of everyone, not just those poor people."

"I—"

But Holmes wasn't finished. His gaze pinned Cruz. "And if you ever turn your comms off and go rogue again, there will be consequences."

"Coward," Santha bit out.

"Enough." Marcus' voice was a deep rasp. His gaze met Cruz's.

They'd been friends long enough that Marcus didn't have to use any words.

"Come on." Cruz swung Santha around, fighting to keep her contained. "We'll meet back here at 0800 for the planning session?"

"Yeah," Marcus said.

Cruz got Santha outside the room and let her go. She rounded on him, her eyes spitting fire. "What the hell—?"

He held up his hands. "I know you're angry."

"I'm leaving."

Those two words make his spine stiffen. "No, you're not."

"You don't get to give me orders, Ramos, I—"

"Come on." He gripped her arm and towed her down the tunnel.

She surprised him by not fighting him. But a terrible tension radiated off her. She was either going to break or explode.

There was one place he went when he needed to burn off the darkness.

He led her into the gym.

A few soldiers were using the treadmills and all lifted a hand in greeting, curious gazes tracing over Santha's long form. Cruz nodded at them and pulled her over to a doorway on the far side the gym. He nudged her inside, closed the door behind them, and locked it.

She studied the open space—covered in rubber mats and ringed with mirrors—with a narrow gaze. "What's this?"

"Private sparring room." Cruz kicked off his boots and stepped out onto the mats. He noted Santha's gaze tracing over his tattoos. "Come on." He made a "come here" gesture with his hand.

"You want to fight?" She raised a dark brow but a light had gone on in her eyes.

"I want you to work off some of that tension before you crack."

Santha toed off her shoes, then moved onto the mats, circling him. "I'm pissed off."

"I got that."

"I really want to be kicking some raptor butt."

He watched her move that long, limber body of hers. "Me, too. But for now, we're grounded until we can recharge and hammer out a plan."

"I could leave," she said again.

Cruz flexed his hands. "You could try."

Her green eyes turned to slits. She sank into a fighting stance, knees loose, arms raised. "You need a reminder that you aren't in charge of me, soldier."

He smiled, anticipation licking his insides. "Bring it."

Chapter Ten

Santha launched herself at Cruz.

She was fueled by all the pent-up emotions swirling inside her, eating at her. She aimed a roundhouse kick at his head. He blocked her and ducked to the side.

She landed, turning as she went, lining up her next kick. He was clearly more powerful than she was, so she needed to use her speed to her advantage.

She landed a chop to his arm, was gratified to hear a grunt, then she aimed a side kick at his knee.

But he was quicker than she'd guessed. He dodged out of her range, grabbed her ankle and twisted.

Santha spun with the move and jerked free. Next, she went in with a punch, feinted and ducked down to swipe at him with her leg.

He was ready though. He leaned forward and grabbed her T-shirt.

She jammed her arms up and broke his hold. When he reached for her again, she let him grab her arm. Then she gripped his thick wrist and used his momentum to pull him over her head.

For a second she didn't think his big body was going to budge, but then he went, falling into a roll and somersaulting away from her.

Santha sprang back onto her feet. She bounced a little, her muscles warm and her blood fired up. She wanted to land some blows, get him to give her a good workout so she could get this shit out of her system.

They both moved at the same time. She launched into a combo of hits and kicks, which he blocked and ducked. They pulled back, both of them breathing heavily. Before he could recover, she took two steps and leaped into the air. Her kick hit his shoulder, knocking him back a step. She followed with a hard punch to his gut.

Damn, the man felt like he was made of rock. She aimed another blow to his side but he blocked with his forearm and she stepped back.

She frowned at him. He was just blocking her, not attacking. "Come on, soldier. Surely you have more than that."

They circled each other and Santha hit him with more kicks and punches. When she stepped back, annoyance was a fiery shimmer in her veins.

"Fight, goddammit. If I wanted a punching bag, I'd go out in the gym."

Cruz's eyes sparked. "I'm not going to hurt you."

"Come on," she urged. "Fight me." She ran in again, and this time her roundhouse kick connected with his chin, snapping his head back.

She pulled back, panting.

He swiped his hand across his mouth, wiping

away a smear of blood. "I'm not going to hit you."

"Then why the hell bother sparring?" She attacked again, her punch landing just above his left kidney. With a curse, he spun away.

"You aren't trying," she spat. "Fight!"

But he let her blows land or glance off him and never lifted a finger against her. Santha felt like she was fighting and he was dancing.

All the anger and horror inside her morphed, turning to a molten emotion she couldn't name...and now all of it was aimed at the man in front of her. If she could purge it, maybe she could think again, breathe again.

Time for something different. She leaped at him, using all her strength and collided with his chest.

He wasn't expecting her change in tactics and he went down, Santha landing on top of him. She pinned his arms down with her knees.

"If you aren't going to give me what I want, then I'll just take it," she said.

He eyed her. "You really want me to smack you around?"

She didn't let herself think. She leaned down and nipped his bottom lip, sinking her teeth in, stealing a hint of his dark, sexy taste.

Cruz's big body went still under her, then his mouth was on hers, forcing her lips open. She clamped her hands either side of his head and kissed him back. It wasn't an easy kiss, nothing gentle or loving about it. It was hard, rough and perfect. His tongue stroked hers and she stroked back, moaning into his mouth. So, so good. She'd always known when she finally had Cruz, it would be better than anything she'd had before.

She reared back, heard his grunt of protest, but as she gripped the neckline of his gray T-shirt and then yanked it over his head and arms, his face changed. It went stark, a hungry glint overtaking those liquid eyes.

The black ink wrapped around his rock-hard biceps and shoulder called her like a siren. She ran her tongue over the design on his arm, tracing the ink.

He groaned. His hand delved into her hair.

"When did you get it?" she asked.

He ripped out the fastening in her hair and it fell down around them.

"After I joined the Marines. It's just ink, but it was my way of reclaiming myself."

"I like it." She nipped at the design on his shoulder.

He jerked his hips and sent them rolling. They tore at each other's clothes. She ripped open his trousers and he made quick work of her shirt. One slash of his big hand had it torn open.

They rolled again and this time he was on top of her. He sank in between her hips and she felt the hard brush of his cock against her. He kissed her, the force of it pushing her head back into the mat.

Cruz wouldn't be an easy lover. He wouldn't be tamed or follow orders.

And dammit, she wanted him. Every stubborn, alpha-male inch of him.

Fucking Cruz would drive every thought out of

her head and leave nothing except the roar of desire. But she wouldn't just roll over and let him do what he wanted.

She lifted her hips and forced him to roll until she was on top again. Her hands attacked his belt and zipper. Then she was yanking his trousers apart and delving under the fitted black cotton of his boxers.

Oh God. Hot hardness filled her hands. His cock was long and thick, pulsing against her skin. She'd feel every inch of him when he filled her.

Santha explored his cock, tracing a thick vein and caressing the rounded head. She loved his long groan.

"Fuck, Santha." The muscles in his neck strained. "You'll be the end of me."

"Oh no, soldier." She pumped him in her hand. "It's just the beginning."

Reluctantly, she released him and stood. It took her three seconds to shimmy out of her trousers and panties. She stood above him completely naked. She didn't have curves or womanly softness. She knew she was hard edges and even harder muscle. But her breasts, while not big, were high and firm and her long legs used to get a few compliments.

Like he read her mind, he skimmed his hands up her calves, the calluses on his fingers scraping over her skin. "Santha."

Just her name. One word. And yet the sexy drawl of his voice expressed that he liked what he saw.

And that hard cock told her even more.

She fell to her knees, lined his cock up beneath her, and sank down in one firm thrust.

"Fuck." His hips reared up, driving him more firmly into her.

God, it hurt more than she anticipated. She stayed still for a second, her hands curled into his hard chest. She was full of him, stretched to the limit. "I'm a little...out of practice."

"*Mi reina*." He cupped her cheeks. "Take a second, get used to me." One of his hands slid down, tracing over her chest, flicking at her nipple, drawing a circle around her belly button. Then it slid between her legs.

At the first brush of his fingers against her clit, she jerked. She moved her hips, wanting more of his touch. He rubbed a slick circle over the nub and she bit her lip at the sensations.

Her gaze flew to his. She saw something in his eyes and she thought it might be satisfaction.

"Move, now," he whispered. "Ride me, *mi reina*."

Santha lifted her hips until just the hard head of him remained inside her, then she slammed down again. He groaned and she pressed her hands flat against his chest and started a wild, rocking rhythm.

She'd wanted to purge the darkness inside.

Now, all she felt was the firestorm of desire and there wasn't room for anything else but Cruz.

***

Dios, she was so fucking beautiful.

Cruz watched, mesmerized, as Santha moved above him. Her breasts jiggled a little and he looked forward to spending more time with them later. He wanted to explore the firm shape of them and taste those dark pink nipples.

He gripped her hips, urging her on as she rode him. His cock moved deep inside her, and she was like a warm, tight glove around him.

Electricity skated down his spine and he felt his body tightening. He'd wanted her for months, had been unable to think of anyone else but her. And now he was deep inside her, watching the fascinating expressions flit across her striking face.

She moved faster and he slid a hand back down between her long thighs. He found that slick, little nub and rubbed it hard. She cried out and he knew her release was building. He couldn't wait to watch her go over. With another inarticulate cry, she started to drive onto him faster and more aggressively.

Cruz slipped his fingers lower, and felt where his cock split her apart. So fucking sexy. He moved back to her clit. Damn, he couldn't wait to have her spread out beneath him, his mouth on her, watching her writhe as he licked and sucked.

"Cruz!" Santha's back arched. Her release hit her and she screamed his name.

He gritted his teeth, wanted to hold on as long as he could. When she finally fell forward on him in a sprawl, he rolled, pinning her beneath him.

"Now it's my turn." He pulled one of her thighs

up and out and he sank more deeply inside her. She moaned, her eyes half open, watching him with a sexy intensity.

The last tiny thread of his control snapped and he hammered inside her. She was hot and so damn wet. He'd never felt anything so good. He thrust again and again until he started to lose his rhythm, his impending release a hot ball at the base of his spine.

With one more thrust, he lodged deep inside her. On a groan, he flooded her with his release.

The orgasm went on and on, and finally, when he was done, he wasn't sure he could hold himself up anymore.

Not wanting to crush her, he slid to the side, falling onto the mat on his back. He threw one arm over his eyes.

"I can't move," Santha said.

He managed to turn his head. Then he grinned. Damned if that wasn't one hell of a beautiful sight. A long, lean and naked Santha sprawled in abandon on the mat, her legs splayed and one arm above her head. Her cheeks were flushed and her eyes were slumberous. He guessed he didn't look much different. "I can't move, either."

She dragged in a deep breath. "Did I wear out the big, bad soldier?"

He snorted. "Wrecked me."

"I wouldn't mind a post-fuck cuddle though. If it's okay with you."

He growled and slid over to her. He rose up on an elbow and loomed over her. "First off, this was more than just a fuck."

She swallowed. "Cruz—"

"No, Santha, be quiet." He yanked her into his arms and lay back with her snuggled tight into his side. Shit, he didn't mind snuggling with a beautiful woman, but it had never felt this good. "Don't ruin the moment by overanalyzing." He stroked her hair, enjoying the scent of her mixed with the musk of their sex.

"Okay," she murmured, pressed her face to his shoulder.

When he felt her mouth moving over his tats, he vowed to himself that he was going to get more. Maybe he'd get her name inked on his chest.

He tangled his hand in her hair. "I mean it. It wasn't just a fuck. If I have to make love to you every day for the next year to prove it to you, I will."

She snorted out a laugh. "How noble of you to make that sacrifice."

He smiled against her hair. "Yeah, that's me, noble." Inside, he wondered why the hell he wasn't freaked out. He'd never made love to a woman. He fucked, he had sex—good sex, hot sex, flirty sex...but not the emotion-filled, loving kind. He cleared his throat. "I should have mentioned it before, but I have a contraceptive implant. All the soldiers do. And I haven't been with anyone since my last checkup, which I passed with flying colors."

"You are noble." She smiled. "Thanks for letting me know. And I don't know what this—" she waved a hand between them "—is, but for now it doesn't need a name." She slowly stroked a hand down the center of his chest.

Miraculously, he felt his nerve endings fire and his cock twitch.

She nipped his shoulder. "I think you should show me again the difference between fucking and what we just did."

Cruz stood up, reached down and pulled her up. He grabbed at their clothes which were spread all over the mat.

She watched him. "Where are we going?"

"Back to my quarters. I'm going to make love to you in my bed." Oh, yeah, he couldn't wait to see her in *his* bed, on *his* sheets.

She licked her lips. "Okay."

"And after that, I'm going to fuck you in the shower. Hard, rough and fast." He grinned. "Then you'll know the difference."

Chapter Eleven

Oh God, she was going to come.

Santha's palms pressed into the hard tile of the shower. Behind her, Cruz's hard hands dug into her buttocks as he slammed his cock into her. She threw her head back, felt a fiery, hot knot tying up low in her belly. He was so big, his thick cock sliding against all her nerve endings, stretching her with a pleasure-pain that was addictive.

"Fuck, this is the best view I've seen in a long time." One of his hands slid onto her lower back. "You are so damned gorgeous. I love this dark-golden skin of yours."

No one had ever called her gorgeous. Santha had always been the strong one, the athletic one.

"I'm going to come, Santha." Cruz growled the words. "But you have to come first."

She was so close, skating along the edge. But even as his heavy thrusts rocked into her, she couldn't quite go over.

He gripped her hips, his thrusts turning rougher. "Come for me, Santha. Come on my cock. Let me feel you milking me."

She made a noise in her throat. "I can't."

"You can." He slapped a hand against her ass.

"Touch yourself."

Helpless to ignore his sexy voice and dirty commands, she slid one hand down between her legs, going lower and lower until she felt the thick root of him where he was sawing in and out of her body. God, it was so sexy to feel herself stretched around him. Then she slid her fingers up until she found her clit, swollen and hot, and oh, so sensitive.

She rubbed her finger against the tiny nub, and a mewling sound escaped from her. She kept rubbing, imagining what Cruz looked like as he hammered into her.

"That's my girl," he murmured. "I can feel you tightening around me. Let it come, *mi reina*."

Another flick and another hard thrust from Cruz and her orgasm knocked into her like an avalanche. Her moans echoed in the shower and seconds later, she heard Cruz's groan as he emptied himself inside her.

Santha's legs gave out, but he was there, holding her up. She let him lift her into his arms. God, it was so sexy. No one had ever carried her around—she was too tall and heavy for most men. But he didn't seem to have a problem. Well, with all those hard, roped muscles, she shouldn't be surprised.

He flicked off the shower and set her on her feet outside the stall, before wrapping her in a towel. He swiped another towel over his chest, then hitched it around her hips. After that, he tugged her into his room, sat on the edge of an armchair and pulled her over to stand between his open thighs. Taking the towel, he set to work drying her.

He was maddeningly thorough. She really thought it would be impossible to feel desire after the orgasms he'd just given her. But the feel of the fabric sliding between her legs and his hot hands sliding over skin, sparked a faint stirring in her belly.

He took his time drying her legs, his gaze tracing over her thighs. He skimmed over her flat belly and then he stopped at her breasts, rubbing the towel over her nipples until they tightened into hard peaks.

She moaned. "How are you doing this to me?"

"This is the 'not fucking' part, Santha." He leaned forward and replaced the towel with his mouth. He sucked at her nipple and gently raked it with his teeth.

She caught her hands in his hair, partly to feel the silk of it and partly to find an anchor.

"I don't catch fire like this." Her voice was breathy. "Sex is just easy fun, not this...this..." All-consuming.

"Good. I like knowing only I can do this to you." Definite male satisfaction in his voice.

A laugh escaped her. "Arrogant man."

"You bet." He pressed a kiss between her breasts, then tucked the towel around her. "Come on, I have plans for that long, lovely body of yours."

God. She wouldn't last the night. He'd make her melt into a puddle of lust.

He smiled his trademark sexy grin. "Food, Santha. I'm going to feed you."

Her shoulders sank. "Oh."

He grabbed her hands and tugged her over to the table near a tiny kitchenette. He grasped her hair in one hand and gave a gentle, teasing tug. "Don't worry. After you eat, I'm going to have you again on my bed, my desk, on the floor. Maybe not in that order, but regardless, you're going to lose count of all the orgasms you're going to have."

Her breath caught in her chest. Yep, puddle of lust.

***

Cruz woke in the darkness. It took only a second to realize he was alone in the bed.

The only light in his dark room was the glow from his clock, casting the simple furniture in shadows. The narrow bunk beside him was empty and he distinctly remembered the pleasure of falling asleep with Santha in his arms. He turned on his side and scanned the room.

Saw the shadow of her on the couch.

He rose, naked, and walked over to her.

She was sitting, wrapped in a sheet, her cheek pressed to her upraised knee.

"Bed feels empty without you, *mi reina*."

"I didn't mean to wake you," she said quietly.

He sat beside her. "You're thinking of the lab."

"What else?" She heaved in a breath. "Every time I close my eyes, it's all I can think about. That little girl..." Santha shook her head. "It makes me so angry. I want to kill all those bastard aliens who think they have the right to come here and take something that isn't theirs. And then to make it worse, they think they can do...those atrocities to our people."

"We'll get them out."

"We both know they'll never be the same." A vicious shake of her head. "I want to kill every raptor on the planet. But I'm going to start with the commander."

He stared at her shadowed face. "It won't bring your sister back."

"I know that, Cruz. But it'll help." Her gaze caught his. "It has to help."

He saw she needed to believe that. Like he had to believe that fighting, protecting what was left of humanity, helped atone for his past.

"We'll get them out *and* we'll kill the commander." He reached for her hand and when her fingers twined with his, he felt like he'd won a prize.

They sat quietly for a moment, cloaked by the shadows and the darkness of their thoughts.

"Sometimes I don't know who I am anymore."

The emptiness in her voice made him ache. "You're Santha Kade." He slid his arm across her shoulders and tucked her in close to his side. "And you're mine." He tipped her head back and kissed her.

This kiss wasn't a battle. Wasn't fueled by lust or pain or anger.

It was slow, gentle, tender.

He pulled back and heard her sigh. Then he felt something deep in his belly, something he hadn't felt for a long time. Following his instinct, he rose and grabbed his battered guitar from where it leaned against the wall.

He sat back down, strummed a little, then closed his eyes and played. The song made him think of Santha. Of sex, of strength and courage...of love for a woman. A specific, particular woman. He felt something inside him, something tight and hurting, ease.

When he finished, he raised his head.

She was staring at him. "That was amazing. You play so well."

He shrugged a shoulder and set the guitar aside. "I haven't felt the music for months. You must have inspired my muse." He rose and tugged her with him. "And you've inspired something else." He nipped at her lips. "Come back to bed."

She went with him wordlessly. She followed him down on the bed, dropping the sheet to leave her naked. He'd never get enough of that body or the expressions on her face when he touched her, or of the little sounds she made when she came.

He rolled her under him and started to caress her, slow and steady. Making love, not tearing at each other, not rushing. He ran his lips over her eyelids, her cheekbones, her jaw. He'd worship her and show her how much more there was to life.

As he slid inside her and started to move, he felt her heart beating in time with his. He'd set out to show her what love could be like...and ended up taking the plunge himself.

***

"The Hawks will drop the squad off here." Marcus stood in the middle of the Ops Area with a giant map projection hanging in the air in front of him. He waved a gloved hand and it marked the location. "Roth, your team will land here—" another hand movement and a glowing red mark appeared "—and come in this way from behind the base."

Roth nodded. "Got it."

Santha studied the man. For all his relaxed stance, leaning against the wall, she recognized a warrior. His hawkish face held that intensity, and he had the body of a fighter.

"Hell Squad will go in here." Marcus moved his hands through the air, tracing a path leading in the front of the raptor base. "We'll head straight to the lab." His gaze moved over them, Santha included.

Her hands curled into fists. *We're coming, hold on.*

A woman pushed her way into the room. Santha instantly recognized Doc Emerson.

She thrust her hands on her hips, emphasizing her tightly packed curves. "I'm coming with you."

Gabe shot to his feet. "No. It's too dangerous."

The doctor straightened. "I'm aware of that, but those people need me—"

"You're too valuable."

Santha didn't think she'd heard the usually silent Gabe say that many words all at once before.

Emerson's mouth firmed into a hard line. "Those people have been injured. Moving them without a medical assessment could kill them. *That's* dangerous."

Marcus' gaze shifted between the two. "Last time I checked, I was in charge of this squad." He speared Gabe with a look. "That means I give the orders." He swung around to face the doctor. "And Doc, that means I decide who goes on a mission."

"Marcus—"

He held up a hand to cut her off. "I agree with you." He looked back at Gabe. "The doc is coming."

Gabe's face turned hard as granite, but he dropped back into his chair and folded his arms.

Emerson stepped forward until the projection caught her, casting shadows over her face. "I'll have a medical team on standby. If there are too many injured for me to deal with, we can call them in. When it's safe, of course."

Marcus nodded.

Roth cleared his throat. "You haven't filled your empty squad spot."

Gabe went still as a statue. Santha knew he'd must be thinking of his brother and her heart went out to the hard, silent man. He didn't look like he needed sympathy, but losing Kareena meant she knew what kind of pain it left inside. And from what Cruz had told her, Gabe and his twin brother had been close.

Marcus scowled. "No. None of our recruits have survived their trial runs."

Claudia snorted from the back where she

slouched in a chair. "They've all gotten themselves shot, or they've run away as soon as we've gotten back to base." She grinned. "Can't imagine why."

"Might be your prickly personality scaring them off," Shaw said from beside Claudia.

The woman scowled at the sniper. "Fuck you, Shaw."

"You wish, Frost."

"Enough," Marcus said, his gaze on Roth. "You have someone in mind?"

"Yeah. Guy called Reed. He came in about two weeks ago with a bunch of survivors who'd travelled down from the north. He was a UC Navy SEAL, apparently on leave doing some diving on the Great Barrier Reef when the raptors attacked. He's good in the water and magic with explosives. He's been with Squad Eight, but he's wasted there."

Cruz leaned forward. "We need someone who'll last. We can't keep taking these green recruits out there. Next one's going to end up dead."

From what Santha knew of the SEAL training, you had to be pretty tough to survive it. "We're going to need a good distraction to get into the raptor base. Explosives could do the trick."

Cruz grinned at her. "Lure the raptors out." He winked at her. "I know someone else who's pretty handy with explosives."

"I'm not staying back to blow things up." She *needed* to be the one going into that lab.

"We'll take this Reed," Marcus said.

Roth nodded. "I'll let Eight know. They'll be

sorry to lose him, but since he's going to Hell Squad, they'll get over it."

Marcus eyed Santha. "You going to follow orders?"

She stiffened. Shit, she felt like she was in her captain's office getting a dressing-down. "I'll do what I think is right."

Marcus shook his head. "Not good enough. You have to follow orders or you don't come."

She gritted her teeth. "Fine."

Beside her, Cruz gripped her arm and squeezed.

Marcus made a closed fist with his hand and the map projection closed. "Everyone suit up. We'll meet at the landing pads in one hour."

Chapter Twelve

Cruz felt the familiar vibration of the Hawk beneath his feet. He gripped an overhead hand hold and watched the rest of Hell Squad as they went through their familiar pre-mission rituals.

Claudia checked her weapons, three times. Shaw was cleaning his sniper rifle. Gabe sat, still and silent, at the back of the quadcopter. Marcus stood near the cockpit, talking quietly with the pilot. Cruz knew their fearless leader would be running scenarios in his head, mapping out every step of the mission.

Doc Emerson was also aboard. She looked wrong dressed in armor and not in her usual lab coat. She wore a streamlined black backpack that contained her medical supplies. Her face was set and she looked ready for anything.

Santha was at the side of the copter, staring out the window at the ruined city below. She was silent but he sensed the edginess radiating off her.

She was ready for this mission.

There was also one new addition to the squad.

Reed MacKinnon was tall and had the lean build of a swimmer. Cruz guessed from the man's tanned skin and sun-bleached brown hair that he liked the outdoors. So far, he hadn't said much, but he seemed relaxed and focused all at once. A good sign. He'd also brought his own modified carbine called a mayhem—with a lightweight missile launcher attached.

Cruz moved closer to Santha and followed her gaze out the window. The ravaged city spread as far as he could see. It was far too easy to only see death and destruction. To mourn what was lost and know that nothing would ever be the same. Too many had died. Too much of what had once been "normal" life would never return.

That was what he'd seen the last few months, all he'd been able to see.

But now there were patches of vibrant green below, where plant life was flourishing. A flock of birds soared and dipped with the wind.

Life was fighting to survive.

His gaze moved to Santha's set face, with her high cheekbones and lush lips. It was what he wanted for her. She could have her revenge, see if the blood of the raptor commander would fill that gaping hole inside her, but Cruz wanted her to live.

He'd had her now. Tasted her. She was in his blood.

She turned her head and caught his gaze. She smiled at him.

Something in his chest loosened.

"We'll be landing in three minutes," Marcus called out. "Everybody hang on."

"Ready?" Cruz asked her.

"Ready."

They landed on the roof of an office building not far from the school. Marcus slid the Hawk door open. "Hell Squad, let's move."

Moments later, Hell Squad was pounding down the stairs and heading in the direction of the raptor base.

They moved into a light jog. Gabe was on point, his gun up, and Claudia brought up the rear. The team made sure Emerson was protected in the center. Cruz kept half of his attention on Reed. The man held his mayhem with practiced ease and moved with a fluid confidence. So far, so good.

They reached a building several hundred meters back from the one Cruz and Santha had used on their recon mission. The squad moved into position on the roof, and Marcus crouched and lifted his binocs.

Then he let out a string of curses.

Cruz had been with Marcus long enough to know that it meant big trouble. "What is it?"

"The raptors are moving out. They're loading supplies into those damn vehicles of theirs."

"What?" Santha snatched up her own binocs and focused on the school buildings.

She didn't say anything but the tightness in her jaw spoke volumes.

She lowered the binocs. "We have to go in. Now."

"We don't know if the prisoners are still there." Marcus cursed. "They could have moved them already."

Shit, Cruz knew it was a bad situation. They could go in, risk the team, and find nothing. Or they could go in and rescue the humans, and still risk the team by dropping directly in a hornet's nest of raptor activity.

But he knew Marcus.

"They're still there," Santha said. "They have to be. We *have* to go in."

A muscle ticked in Marcus' jaw. "We go in."

***

Santha tried to keep her hands from twitching on her crossbow as she watched the raptors continue to load up supplies.

"Reed, you're up," Marcus said. "We need a good diversion."

"You'll get one." The tall man caught Santha's gaze and gave her a small nod. He had rugged outdoorsman stamped all over him—from his athletic body to his tanned skin. When you added a square jaw covered in sexy stubble, hazel eyes and shaggy hair tipped gold at the ends, and she figured he didn't lack for feminine company. As he slipped away, it was hard not to admire his easy grace.

She looked away and saw Cruz scowling at her.

Her chest tightened. That was the face that really did it for her. Sex and sin wrapped up in a lean, dark package she wanted to lick all over. She winked at him.

His scowl melted away into a reluctant smile. Then together, they turned back to watch the raptors.

They waited. None of the Hell Squad members moved. They stayed still, watchful.

Santha felt like she was going to explode. She hated waiting. She wanted to aim her crossbow and take down as many of the aliens below as she could. She wanted—no, needed—to storm into that building and see if those people were still there. To find that little girl and get her out.

God, what if they had been moved? Her mouth went dry. They'd have to start all over again in the search, and who knew how many of them would be dead by then.

A boom shattered the late-morning stillness.

They all looked north.

A huge blue ball rose into the air and then the heart of it turned a brilliant red. Her pulse jumped. Jesus, Reed was using Backfire explosives.

The secondary explosion detonated, and the shockwave hit them.

Cruz slammed into her, his big body curling around hers. Holy Hell, she'd never seen Backfires used before. She'd only heard of them. They could do a lot of damage, had good pyrotechnics, but the effects were mostly localized.

Which was why they all hadn't been blasted into tiny pieces.

Santha had barely caught her breath when another huge explosion rocked them. This one was a standard charge. The ground under them vibrated, and a cloud of black smoke rose in the air.

The raptors in the yard below exploded into a chaotic frenzy. One of the raptors appeared to be yelling out orders, and suddenly two thirds of the aliens headed off in the direction of Reed's explosions.

"The guy is *good*," Shaw murmured from nearby.

Santha studied the remaining raptors. Still a large number of them, but it would have to do. She'd had worse odds before.

Cruz touched her shoulder and she felt the burn of his hand even through her borrowed body armor. A silent good luck.

"Emerson, you stay back until I signal you." Marcus pinned the doctor with a glare.

"Got it."

"Hell Squad," Marcus said, "time to do what we do best. Ready to go to hell?"

"Hell, yeah!" all the team responded. "The devil needs an ass-kicking!"

The team exploded into action.

Santha stayed back beside Shaw. His sniper rifle was like an extension of him as he worked to take down as many raptors as he could.

Santha's crossbow sang in her hands as she sent bolt after bolt into the raptors below.

The rest of the team charged across the yard. Marcus and Cruz worked in tandem, never pausing in firing their carbines. Claudia had a thermo shotgun that boomed when she fired, and Gabe was hot on her heels with his weapon.

They hit the oncoming wave of raptors.

Santha watched Cruz slam into an enormous raptor. Her heart was pounding double-time, but she kept her cool and took down two more raptors trying to get to him. Cruz strained against the alien before getting his gun up. The raptor's head exploded and its body slumped to the ground.

She released the breath she was holding.

Marcus was...brutal. His blood-splattered face was intense as he took out raptor after raptor. Gabe was just plain scary. He'd switched to two combat knives and he moved so fast the blades were barely visible. He sliced and stabbed anything in his path. No man could move that fast.

Claudia moved with an elegance Santha hadn't expected from the tough, non-nonsense woman. She pressed a boot to a raptor's belly and he fell backward. She lifted her shotgun and showed no mercy.

Soon, the remaining raptors were pulling back behind their line of vehicles and into a building across from the school to regroup.

"Let's move." Marcus' gravelly voice came through Santha's earpiece clearly.

In unison, she and Shaw slid over the edge of the roof to the ground below. Shaw helped Emerson down. They hurried down the street and across the body-strewn schoolyard, joining the others.

Santha moved up close to Cruz and ran an assessing eye over him. He pressed a gloved finger to her cheek, then nodded toward the building. As a group, the squad moved up the steps and into the building.

Inside, it took a second for her vision to adjust from full sun to the dim light. Santha slung her crossbow onto her back and pulled out her laser pistols.

Marcus held up a fist and, as one, the group stopped in their tracks. Waited. Listened.

Everything was silent.

Santha swallowed. No moans or cries. Nothing.

They moved quickly, clearing rooms.

"Too fucking quiet," Cruz said.

"Usually means a shitstorm is coming," Shaw muttered. "Just how we like it."

They moved down the long, main corridor.

A noise. A scratching sound.

They paused.

"What the hell is that?" Claudia's face was pressed to her scope as she swung her carbine around.

"I'm sure we're about to find out," Marcus growled.

Ahead, out of the darkness, came a snarl.

And the sound of claws on wood.

In the next second, the hall filled with canids. Some were running full-tilt toward them, others were slinking along the ceiling, their red gazes trained on Hell Squad.

"Here doggy, doggy," Shaw said softly, lining up his rifle.

He took down three canids in quick succession. Santha tossed a grenade filled with her anti-canid spray. It exploded, spraying the aliens with a fine mist of the cedar oil mixture. As the lead animals started howling in pain, she swung her pistols up and shot them.

But more rushed forward and leaped onto the team.

Marcus and Cruz worked shoulder to shoulder, cutting through the dog-like aliens with laser fire. Behind them, Claudia and Gabe had switched to knives. They sliced and hacked.

As Santha kept firing, she understood how the team had gotten its name. Soon, they all stood in a blood-smeared hall, surrounded by the bodies of dozens of canids.

"I hate these things." Gabe gave one animal a kick before cleaning his knife on its hide.

"Come on," Marcus said. "Let's get to the lab and then get out of here."

It took a few more minutes and they reached the door that led to the lab. Santha swallowed against the large lump in her throat. There was no noise from behind the door.

Cruz pushed it open.

At first, Santha thought the lab was empty.

But then she saw the shapes of bodies lying still and quiet in their beds. *No. No!*

She rushed inside.

"Santha!" Cruz was right behind her, checking the room for threats. The rest of the team dashed behind them.

She reached the first bed. A man in his mid-thirties lay there, his eyes closed. But his chest was moving. Her shoulders sagged. He was alive.

Then she saw the tube going from his arm to some sort of bag on a stand beside him. It was filled with a yellow sludge that was slowly working its way inside him.

"Doc?" Marcus said.

Emerson moved forward and checked the man's vitals. "He's alive. Barely." She lifted her m- scanner, then cursed under her breath. "Poison." She yanked the tube out. "They're being euthanized. Go, get the tubes out!"

The team moved fast, each one going to pull the tubes from the patients.

Santha moved beside a boy in his teens. She pulled the tube out of his arm...and the end of it moved. She gasped. It was part organic and the end had a mouth like a leech, which puckered as if it were looking to suck onto something. She dropped it on the floor and stamped on it.

The boy was frighteningly pale. His eyes were open, and he stared blankly up at the ceiling.

Her heart heavy, she hurried along, pulling out more tubes.

The last bed held a body that was smaller than the rest. Santha's heart pounded in her chest. "Oh no."

It was the little girl they'd seen before. Her eyes were closed and she was so, so still. Santha pulled the tube out of her arm and pressed a hand to the girl's cheek.

Cold. Too cold.

"Doc? Doc, can you help!"

Emerson ran over, and as she checked for vital signs, the girl moved, her eyes opening. They were covered in a milky white film.

"She's alive. I've no idea what damage they've

done to her brain, but right now she's in deep shock." Emerson fitted a snug, stretchy cap over the girl's head. "That'll cover her wounds until I can treat her back at base."

"I'll take her." Cruz appeared and lifted the girl into his arms. Santha's insides warmed at the sight of the big, tough muscled soldier gently cradling the tiny, young girl.

Santha turned and watched the rest of the squad opening up the field iono-stretchers they'd brought. Each small box opened out to produce a canvas hammock between the ends. They used electrohydrodynamics to produce the thrust that kept a loaded stretcher in the air without needing an engine. They were lightweight and easy to maneuver with no more than a slight push.

"Eight patients dead and ten still alive," Emerson said, her face grim.

Marcus nodded and touched his earpiece. "Elle, we've found survivors. Heading out now."

"Roger that, Marcus. Did you find the scientists?"

Marcus looked over at Doctor Emerson. She was checking the final patients who were still alive.

"No sign of Dr. Lonsdale. It's likely he's dead."

Marcus cursed. "And the other? Dr. Vasin?"

"That's me," a quiet, shaky voice said. Santha could hear the light strains of a Russian accent.

Santha turned and saw a woman so painfully thin her cheekbones and collarbones were pressed hard against her skin. Her dark hair had been shorn off. As Marcus helped her onto the stretcher,

Santha noted the threadbare clothes and a blood-soaked bandage covering her chest.

Doc Emerson gently pushed the woman down. "Just rest. It's Natalya, right? We're going to get you out of here."

"Randall's dead?"

"We aren't sure. But he's not here."

The woman sighed. "He wasn't doing well. He kept holding on, hoping his wife was still alive. But the...aliens removed some of his organs—" The woman shuddered.

"Just be quiet now," Santha said, trying for a soothing tone.

The woman reached out and grabbed Santha's arm, squeezing with a surprising strength. "There are others."

Santha frowned, a horrible feeling rising inside her. "Others?"

"Other human guinea pigs," Dr. Vasin said. "They were here but the aliens moved them somewhere else. Maybe Randall was with them. Some of these people here also spoke of another lab. A larger one."

Chapter Thirteen

Fuck. Cruz couldn't believe what he was hearing. "Where?"

The scientist dropped back on her stretcher, sagging with exhaustion. "I don't know."

The little girl stirred in Cruz's arms. "Broken bridge." Her nose wrinkled. "Scary face."

She'd spoken! The surprise Cruz felt at hearing the little girl's voice was interrupted when Elle's voice sounded in his ear.

"Marcus, you have incoming raptors. Reed led them on a merry chase, but they've just left the explosion site and are coming back. Looks like they've been joined by another raptor team."

"Okay, Elle." Marcus gripped two stretchers and started moving toward the door. "We have to go. Now."

They hurried through the corridors. Santha pushed a man's stretcher ahead of her and dragged Dr. Vasin's behind. Cruz clutched the girl in his arms.

They reached the door and stepped into the fierce midday sun.

There was a whoosh of air and a ship appeared

148

above them like a giant bird of prey.

Shit. "Ptero!" Cruz yelled.

He tightened his grip on the tiny slip of a girl and watched as the raptor ship swiveled in the air above them. On the ground, raptors poured into the yard.

Too many. His gut turned to rock. There were too many.

Suddenly, something flew off the roof of the neighboring building and slammed into the ptero. An explosion engulfed the alien ship and it veered sharply to the left, flying overhead before slamming into the building behind them with an earsplitting crunch of rock and metal.

Ahead, Cruz saw Reed leap off the roof from where he'd fired the missile, his mayhem over his shoulder.

Raptors were running toward them, firing their weapons.

Cruz shoved the girl at Santha. "Pull the patients back behind cover." He raced with his teammates to meet the enemy.

He didn't have time to watch if Santha followed orders, but he knew she'd do anything to keep those people safe. He yanked his carbine off his shoulder and started firing.

It didn't take long for Hell Squad to thin the raptors out. The remaining aliens ducked for cover or ran.

Marcus waved the team into cover behind an overturned van. "We need an escape route, Elle."

"Working on it. We can't risk a Hawk landing at

the school, so you need to get some distance between you and the raptors. Round everyone up and head out the western gate."

Cruz swiveled and eyed the gate in the fence across a small playing field. "We can make it."

Marcus and Cruz jogged over to Santha. The little girl was standing beside her and Santha was cursing. A stretcher had been damaged by the gunfire and Dr. Vasin had spilled onto the ground.

Santha scraped a hand over her head. "I can't fix it."

"Don't worry." Reed muscled in and scooped the scientist up. "I'll carry her."

"All right, Hell Squad. Grab a stretcher or a patient and let's get out of here." Marcus took the lead, dragging two stretchers behind him.

Cruz grabbed the girl again and she clung to him like glue. They were moving quickly, but behind them, Cruz heard canids howling. More raptors were coming.

They'd left the school and were moving down the street when ahead, a team of raptors stepped out and blocked their route.

"Fuck," Cruz muttered.

"That's a really naughty word," the girl said.

Cruz blinked. There was clearly nothing wrong with her hearing. He cleared his throat and focused on the threat. "Options?"

Marcus' jaw was tight. "We're out of them."

Suddenly, five Darkswifts flew overhead, each glider a slim-line, dark shadow against the sky.

The lasers mounted on the front of the gliders

opened fire on the raptors below, cutting them down.

"Woo-hoo!" Shaw punched a hand in the air.

"Thought you guys might need a little assistance," Roth's voice drawled through the earpiece.

Squad Nine had arrived.

"Come on, Hell Squad, let's get out of here." Marcus waved them onward.

They all started moving again when the distinctive shape of a velox slinked out of a building ahead.

"Shit," Cruz muttered.

"That's naughty, too," the girl murmured.

"You have to keep moving." Santha nudged her stretcher toward Cruz. "Take them and get to the Hawk. I'll hold this thing off."

"No." Dammit, she couldn't take it on alone. He wouldn't stand by and watch her die.

"I'll help." Claudia nudged her stretcher toward Reed and stepped up, shoulder to shoulder with Santha. She glanced at the team. "Go."

Santha moved in close to Cruz. "Don't worry, soldier." She pressed a quick kiss to his lips. "You've given me a very good reason to stick around."

He savored the brief hint of her taste, then tightened his arms around the little girl. Dammit, he wanted to stay and help fight. But he had to get these people to safety. Santha wouldn't forgive him if he didn't.

But he couldn't turn away. It seemed none of the

team could. Like they were hypnotized, Cruz and the rest of Hell Squad watched the two woman advance on the creature. Both of them were strong, and while Santha was taller and leaner than Claudia—who was all solid muscle and a bad attitude—she was no less deadly.

They were both holding two guns. Santha's Shockwaves made a distinctive sound as they fired. Claudia was a pro at using her carbine and her laser pistol in tandem.

The lasers tore into the creature, but barely seemed to affect it. Its powerful muscles bunched, then it let out a high-pitched screech and rushed at the women.

Quick as lightning, Santha and Claudia dropped their guns and drew their combat knives.

The velox kept coming. Its red eyes glowed— blazing with hunger and rage.

Cruz's stomach went tight, but as the creature advanced, the women moved together in a lethal dance.

"Holy shit," Shaw said from beside Cruz, his eyes wide. "Fucking poetry in motion."

They were. The women worked together, using each other to distract and attack. One would draw the alien out, while the other would slide in to cut and stab at the creature's softer underbelly.

Blood slicked down the sides of the velox and Santha and Claudia never stopped moving.

"We have to go." Marcus said, bringing Cruz back to reality.

He wanted to curse, but he thought he'd get

another reprimand from the girl. With one last glance at his woman, he followed the rest of his team.

Elle came on the line. "In another few hundred meters you'll see a paved area with a fountain. The Hawk's landing there now."

They hustled toward the Hawk and every step of the way, Cruz thought of Santha. Was she okay? Had they killed it? Had it managed to hit her?

She'd survived a long time alone, doing very dangerous things. He knew she'd be fine and she'd kick his ass for worrying so much.

Didn't make it any easier, though.

They rounded a corner and spotted the Hawk. As they neared, the side door slid open and Finn appeared, waving them in.

They loaded the patients in. Those well enough to sit were strapped into seats. Emerson moved between the stretchers, locking them into place and checking on the occupants. The girl was looking glassy-eyed and lethargic. Cruz was starting to worry something else might be wrong with her. He tried to set her down on one of the seats in the Hawk.

"No." She clung to him, her face filled with terror.

"You're safe now. Sit here and we'll take off soon."

She clamped her thin arms and legs around him and shook her head.

Cruz glanced up and saw Reed was having similar trouble with Dr. Vasin. The woman was clinging to him like her survival depended on it.

Shit. Cruz didn't want the girl to panic or for him to hurt her, so he gave in with a sigh. He tucked her head against his shoulder. "All right. Just hold on, okay?"

Another nod. One that made something warm glow in his chest.

Across from him, Reed sat, cradling Dr. Vasin to him.

Cruz shifted a little so he could glance at his watch. Santha and Claudia still weren't back.

Marcus was standing at the side of the Hawk, one arm gripping the doorframe above his head. He was scowling.

Cruz knew they couldn't risk sitting here too long. The raptors would send reinforcements.

Where the hell were Santha and Claudia?

"We need to get going, Marcus," Finn called out from the cockpit.

"One more minute," Marcus barked back. "We don't leave anyone behind."

Cruz knew Marcus wouldn't leave the women. Hell, Cruz had seen him disobey direct commands to make sure they never left a man behind, but, Cruz glanced at the girl, they couldn't risk these innocent people's lives.

"They'll be here," Shaw said from behind Cruz.

But the sniper had a worried look on his face.

Just then, Santha and Claudia sprinted out from around the building. Cruz's heart knocked against his ribs. They were both splattered in blood, but they were alive.

Then he saw what was chasing them.

The rex was taller than the buildings around them. It stomped on out onto the street on its massive clawed feet. Then it arched its neck, gave an earsplitting roar and flashed sharp teeth as long as Cruz's forearm.

"Finn, take off," Marcus shouted.

What? Santha and Claudia were still meters away. "Marcus—"

He shot Cruz a hot look. "Stay two meters off the ground. Once Santha and Claudia are aboard, get us out of here. Fast."

The Hawk lifted. Ahead, Claudia was running, arms pumping. Santha was two meters behind her. As Claudia neared, she leaped into the air. Shaw reached out, grabbed her arm, and hauled her in.

Santha did the same, taking a graceful leap. Marcus grabbed her, and a second later she was in the Hawk.

"Go!" Marcus roared.

The rex roared as well, picking up speed.

The Hawk shot upward fast, then spun, rising higher and higher. Air roared past the still-open door.

Below, the rex, robbed of its meal, turned in frustrated circles and stamped its feet.

Santha's gaze hit Cruz's. She was panting, her hair soaked with sweat and blood. Damn, he still thought she looked beautiful.

She moved over to him, ran a hand gently over the girl's head, then reached up and yanked his face to hers.

Alive. As she kissed the hell out of him, that was all Cruz could think. She was beating with life and passion and courage, and he wanted more of it.

***

Santha paced the tunnel outside the infirmary.

Doc Emerson and her team had been in there for what felt like forever, working on the rescued prisoners.

The rest of Hell Squad waited with Santha, everyone still in their armor and wearing the bloody remnants of their battle. She walked past Cruz standing with his arms crossed over his chest and leaning against the wall. Then past Shaw and Claudia, who were bickering about something to do with thermo bullets and reload speeds. Santha had spent enough time with them now to know it was their way to deal with the tension. And on top of that, they seemed to enjoy it. Gabe was watching them and shaking his head.

Santha stopped, swiveled and glanced at the infirmary door. *Come on, open.* She paced back the way she'd come.

She reached Marcus, where he stood with his arms wrapped around Elle. He was talking quietly with Reed. Santha guessed from the fact that Reed wasn't injured, and hadn't run off screaming, that he'd made the cut as a member of Hell Squad.

Elle cleared her throat. "I just wanted you all to know I asked Noah to work on finding the location of the second lab. He's scouring Santha's data again and cross-referencing with drone feed. As soon as he has something, he'll let us know."

Santha traded a dark glance with Cruz. The longer it took, the more people who would suffer...die. Dammit to hell.

Suddenly, the door opened. Santha stopped in her tracks and felt the tension spike in the rest of the squad.

Emerson looked three steps beyond exhausted. The doctor's blonde hair was damp at the temples and she had a smear of blood on one cheek. Dark circles underscored her eyes.

"We lost one," she said quietly.

Santha's heart spasmed. *Oh, God. Please, not the little girl.*

Emerson released a long breath. "He was too far gone. The damage those bastards had inflicted was too extensive." She managed a wan smile. "The others are all stabilized."

Marcus clapped a big hand on the doctor's shoulder. "Good job, Doc."

"Can we see them?" Reed asked.

"Yes. But keep the visits quick. Many of them are sedated."

Santha stepped forward, felt Cruz's arm brush hers as he joined her. "The girl?"

The doctor's smile widened. "Her name's Bryony. She's eating ice cream."

Santha laughed. "Really?"

"Yep. I've removed the wiring the raptors left in her, but I still need to do more scans to assess the damage." Doc Emerson's mouth tightened. "For now, she seems fine." The doctor's gaze moved to Cruz. "She'd like to see you both."

Santha and Cruz shuffled into the infirmary. Most of the patients were tucked into the row of bunks, sedated and sleeping. Dr. Vasin sat on her bunk, her knees to her chest and her thin arms wrapped around them.

Bryony, dressed in a fresh infirmary gown, sat on a stool at a nearby table, spooning ice cream so fast into her mouth, Santha was worried she'd get brain freeze. The girl looked up, spotted them, then gave them a shy smile.

"How are you feeling?" Santha asked, wanting to touch her but not wanting to scare her.

"The ice cream is yummy." She set the spoon down and ran a self-conscious hand over her uneven hair.

Santha made a mental note to see about finding someone who could cut it for her. Emerson had covered the girl's head wounds with small med-patches. Santha really hoped the nano-meds could repair the damage.

Cruz tweaked the girl's nose. "Glad you're doing better. I think you'll like it here."

Bryony nodded. "There are lots of flavors of ice cream. The doctor said I have to stay here for now. Until she fixes me all up." The girl tilted her head. "Will you stay with me?" Her gaze was all for Cruz this time.

Santha smothered a smile. She could hardly blame the girl for falling into hero worship for the big, strong man who'd saved her.

"We have to go." Cruz tipped the girl's chin up. "I have more people to help."

She considered for a second. "Okay."

"But I have some friends, their names are Leo and Clare. I thought they could visit you."

"Are they old?"

Cruz's lips quirked. "Not like me. They're just a bit older than you." He tweaked her nose again. "Santha and I will come and see you as soon as we get back."

Bryony's green eyes clouded. "You're going after them? The other people who are trapped?"

Santha nodded. "We will. But first we have to find them."

"Good." Bryony wrapped her arms around her middle. "It's horrible with…them." The last word came out as a tortured whisper.

Cruz touched her cheek. "We don't know where the lab is, but we'll work non-stop until we find it." It was a promise Cruz vowed to keep.

"Remember, it's under the broken bridge." Bryony shuddered. "I hated that scary face."

This time, Santha let herself touch the girl, tucking a strand of hair behind her ear. "You don't have to worry about anything scary anymore. We'll see you when we get back."

Together, Santha and Cruz strode out of the infirmary. On the way out, Santha saw Reed sitting next to Dr. Vasin, murmuring quietly to her.

"Lots of broken bridges in a city built on a harbor," Cruz said.

"Yes, but it gives us somewhere to start."

"Let's go grab a quick shower and then give Elle and Noah a prod."

Santha nodded at Cruz's suggestion. At least they'd be doing *something*.

Chapter Fourteen

Santha stalked down the tunnel towards Cruz's quarters. She was frustrated, tired and edgy all at once.

She'd hung over Noah and Elle's shoulders until Noah had threatened to physically toss her out of his computer lab if she didn't leave. Santha sniffed. Damn, the man was grumpy. She'd only been trying to help find the location of the damn lab.

Cruz had disappeared an hour ago. Santha wondered if she could talk him into another sparring match.

She reached his door and pressed her palm to the lock. He'd told her he'd asked Noah to program her in. It beeped and the door opened.

The smell that hit her made her stomach clench and her mouth water. She smelled spices that made her think of family and better times. Turmeric, coriander and cumin.

She stepped inside. "What's going on?"

Cruz looked up from where he stood at the tiny stove in the kitchenette. He held a large spoon in one hand. "I've made us dinner."

An unidentifiable emotion rose up and clamped around her throat. This man, a battle-hardened soldier, had made her favorite meal. One she hadn't tasted in over a year. She just stared at him.

He shifted self-consciously under her scrutiny and waved the spoon. "Come and try it. I had to beg the chef for the spices. I wasn't sure of the exact amounts so I had to wing it a bit. And I managed to get some real chicken." He grimaced. "I won't tell you what I had to promise Old Man Hamish in return."

"Old Man Hamish?"

"He runs the hydroponic garden and also keeps a few chickens. Guards them like they lay golden eggs. Anyway, I didn't want to ruin this by using protein substitute."

Santha swallowed the lump in her throat and moved up beside him. In the pan, succulent pieces of chicken simmered in the sauce with a variety of vegetables. "It smells perfect."

"How are Noah and Elle doing?"

Santha screwed up her nose. "Nothing yet. They're running searches and cross referencing information…but they said it'll take time." Time those poor people didn't have.

Cruz grabbed her shoulder, squeezed. "We'll find it." He pulled away to stir the pan. "I checked on Bryony. She was sleeping."

Probably the first real sleep she'd had in a long time. Santha tried to focus on the girl and the others they had managed to rescue.

The auto-oven beeped. Cruz grabbed a kitchen towel and opened it. He pulled out a small tray of chapattis.

Now she was truly speechless.

He pulled a face. "I can't claim the credit for these. Chef made them after I pleaded pitifully...there might have even been a bit of begging."

"Cruz—"

He smiled and nudged her toward the two-seater table. "Sit."

She did, and watched him serve up the meal. She tried the curry with an undeniable mix of trepidation and excitement, and, while it mightn't have tasted exactly like Kareena's, it was good. The best curry she'd had in a long time.

Santha reached out and grabbed his hand. "Thank you."

Cruz looked up from his meal. "You're welcome." He broke off a piece of chapatti. "You know, I fully expect you to make me tamales sometime."

She shook her head as she took another mouthful of curry. "I'd probably kill you. Cooking is not my best skill."

His eyes warmed. "Well, luckily, you have plenty of other skills to make up for it."

They finished their meal and Santha couldn't remember the last time she'd felt so relaxed.

Then she remembered the lab and tension crept back in like a thief in the night.

Cruz must have noticed, because he stood and nodded his head toward the small seating area. "Come curl up on the couch."

Santha watched him walk over to the living space. His worn jeans hugged his damn fine ass, and his T-shirt stretched hard over his muscles. She felt a lick of heat inside. She didn't think she'd ever get tired of watching him.

When he picked up the guitar from the corner, she smiled. "You going to serenade me?"

He settled on the coffee table in front of her and positioned the beaten-up instrument on his lap. "Something like that." His gaze traced over her face. "My muse seems to be back with a vengeance."

Santha's pulse jumped.

His hot gaze speared into her. "I feel the music again." He started strumming.

Santha felt the music wash over her. She watched, entranced, as he leaned over the instrument and made music that caused goose bumps to flicker over her skin. His Latin heritage was obvious in the sound, conjuring up images of twirling women in colorful skirts, or sexy lovers moving against each other.

As he played, all the thoughts and worries and concerns drained from her head. Santha knew it was nothing more than a temporary reprieve, but she'd take it.

He moved onto a different song. She thought about closing her eyes, but she really liked watching him. The way his big hands moved so competently over the strings. The way he moved his head to the music, lost in the magic.

The next song was so sexy, it sent a languid warmth through her body. And made her want to dance.

With him, she felt comfortable enough to shake off some inhibitions. She stood. She hadn't danced in what felt like forever. Since the last time Kareena had dragged her out to a club for a girls' night out. The thought of Kareena laughing and dancing to a frantic beat made Santha smile.

Santha tugged the tie out of her hair. The dark locks fell over her shoulders. Then she swayed to the rhythm, finding the beat. She raised her hands and closed her eyes. Feeling what he poured into the music deep down to her bones.

Santha did a slow turn and opened her eyes.

He was watching her with an intensity that stole her breath. There was sex and desire and other unnamable emotions in the deep brown of his eyes. Heat flashed through her.

"Take off your clothes," he murmured.

Another wave of heat, this one strong enough to make her legs feel weak. She lifted a hand to the buttons on her shirt and flicked the first one open.

As she worked her way down the row of buttons, his gaze remained glued to her hand. He didn't falter on the music and she smiled. Oh, but she wanted his full attention.

She shrugged her shoulders and the shirt fell to the floor. She unsnapped her trousers and kicked them off. As she stood there in simple, black cotton underwear, she wished she owned something lacy, something sexier.

"*Mi reina.*" But his voice and those eyes made her realize he didn't really care what she wore.

Still swaying to the music, she unclipped her bra

and dropped it to the floor. She cupped her breasts and watched his eyes flare.

God, she felt...powerful. Powerful and desired.

She slipped her thumbs in the sides of her panties, then leaned over and tugged them down her legs. Then, completely naked, she resumed her dancing. Dancing for him.

Cruz's face looked stark, the desire in his eyes like a firestorm. "You are so fucking sexy."

He kept playing and she kept dancing, the tension stretching tight between them.

"Touch yourself." His voice was a low growl.

Biting her lip, Santha let a hand drift down her belly. She slipped her fingers between her legs and found her clit. "Oh."

This time, his fingers messed up, striking a bad note on the guitar.

He muttered a curse and set the instrument aside. "I'm going to eat you now. And I'm not going to stop until you come on my tongue."

Her lower body spasmed. She watched him stride towards her, every part of her filled with electricity.

He pushed her back into the armchair, then he kneeled between her legs. His big hands pushed her thighs apart, baring her to him. He made a humming noise and pressed his mouth to her.

"Cruz!" Her hips jerked upward. The sensation was...indescribable.

He worked her hard. He lapped at her, sucked on her clit, his tongue stabbing into her, not letting up until she was sobbing his name. Her orgasm crashed over her, her back arching.

Then he stood, tore his clothes off and scooped her up.

He set her on her feet and bent her away from him until she pressed her palms flat on the seat of the chair. When his hand curved over her buttock, she pushed back against him. "Yes."

Cruz pumped into her with one hard thrust.

A groan escaped her throat.

"Tilt your hips," he growled. "Take more of me."

She thrust back against him, their bodies slapping together. It felt so good to be filled up by him. It was so raw, so real.

"Damn, *mi reina*, I could fuck your forever." His guttural voice rasped over her ear.

Her skin tightened, her nipples hard as pebbles. She felt her release coming, growing to frightening proportions. "Harder."

His fingers bit into her ass and his other hand slipped over her belly. He used his fingers to spread her open and found her clit. She thrashed against him.

"That's it, *bella*." His mouth grazed the side of her neck. "Come for me now."

And she did. She screamed so loud she was sure his neighbors would be complaining in the morning.

A second later, he groaned and his cock pulsed inside her. He buried his face against her neck and growled out her name.

***

Damn, he felt good.

As Cruz moved around the tiny kitchenette, making breakfast, and deliberately rubbing up against Santha at every opportunity, he felt on top of the fucking world.

He'd made love to Santha until they'd both been exhausted and he'd slept well with her wrapped up in his arms. Perfect.

And now she was here, in his space, and while she was dressed in cargo trousers and a T-shirt, her hair was mussed and her face relaxed. She was even humming under her breath.

She set some slightly singed eggs down on the table. "Breakfast is served."

He brought over two glasses of protein drink and raised a brow at the eggs.

She sat and shrugged. "Told you I wasn't much of a cook." She nibbled on the edge of some toast. "I want to go and check in with Noah and Elle as soon as we're done."

Cruz nodded. "They should have eliminated some of the bridges around the city—"

"Maybe they have a location?"

He shook his head. "They would have called us."

Santha's shoulders sagged. "You're right." She took a bite of eggs. "I thought I might go and visit Bryony. I want to see if there's someone who can cut her hair."

"Liberty," he said. "She takes care of stuff like that. Always has a cloud of blonde hair like she stepped out of a salon."

Santha paused and studied him with a

considering eye. "She's a good…friend of yours?"

Shit. The eggs in his mouth turned to concrete. Liberty liked men, especially soldiers. She was sexy and unafraid of it. Cruz had shared the sheets with her once. He swallowed. "Ah…all I can say is that I only have eyes for you now, *mi reina.*"

Santha's eyes narrowed and she shook her toast at him. "And don't forget that, soldier. I'm rather handy with knives—" a narrow smile "—and if you get forgetful, I may have to pay Ms. Cloud-of-Blonde-Hair a visit…after I'm through with you."

Right. He took a sip of his protein drink, then he grinned. "Damn, you're sexy when you're mean."

She laughed and forked up more food. "I'll track down this Liberty and see if she'll do Bryony's hair. And I want to check and make sure Bryony slept okay. She was talking about broken bridges and scary faces…" Santha stopped, her brow creasing.

When she trailed off, Cruz set his fork down. "What is it?"

"Scary *face.* When Bryony mentioned a scary face, I thought she was just talking about the raptors. But she said face." Santha snapped her fingers. "Luna Park!"

"Luna what?"

"You aren't a local, so you probably don't know about it. There used to be a small, historic amusement park on the northern side of the Harbor Bridge. It's really old. And it has this giant face at the entrance."

Cruz straightened. "We need to check it out."

"Can we get a drone over there? Confirm any raptor activity."

He nodded. "I'll get Elle on it."

An hour later, Cruz stood beside Santha as they watched Elle furiously tapping at her computer and swiping the screen, taking the necessary steps to view the drone feed. Slowly but surely, the rest of Hell Squad had also filed in.

"I don't know why all you grunts have to be in here," Noah grumbled, glancing at the assembled crowd.

"Can it, Kim," Shaw said. "I know you prefer talking to your computer chips and hard drives, but an occasional conversation with an actual human could help your lack of personality."

Noah gave Shaw a bland stare. "You're only proving my point. You standing here all glowering and scowling won't make this go any faster. Don't you have something to shoot or wrestle?"

"Look you—"

They both cut off when the door opened and General Holmes strode in. "You found something."

"One of the rescued prisoners remembered something that narrowed down the location of the raptor lab," Marcus said. "Luna Park."

Holmes looked at Elle. "You have confirmation?"

"I've been running a program to analyze the drone feed of that area." Elle tapped the screen. "Here are the results."

Images filled the screen.

There were raptors all over Luna Park. In every image but one.

Santha gasped. She focused on a slightly blurry picture of a line of humans chained together, being led into a building.

"We're going in," Marcus said in his grit-edged voice.

Holmes' jaw tightened. He opened his mouth—

Santha slashed a hand through the air. "No resting or waiting or planning. While we rested last time, they were killing those people. They know we're onto them now, so there's a good chance they'll start euthanizing other humans as well."

The general raked a hand through his dark hair.

Marcus crossed his arms. "We're going in."

Holmes nodded. "Go. Get them out. And take whatever resources you need."

Chapter Fifteen

The Hawk ride was silent and tense. All of Hell Squad sat silently, mulling over the possibilities of what they would find at Luna Park. Doc Emerson sat in her chair, her hands fiddling with her m-scanner.

Santha stroked her crossbow. Time to end this. She'd help free any prisoners, and then she was going after the commander.

Elle's voice came through their earpieces. "No raptor signatures at the Luna Park location."

Several people cursed and Santha's hand clenched on her weapon.

"There are several human signatures, though," Elle continued.

Santha exchanged a look with Cruz. "Trap?"

"Could be."

Marcus stared at the floor for a second. "Doesn't matter. We have to help those people." He arched his neck to look into the cockpit. "Finn, don't bother dropping us too far away. If this is a trap, they know we're coming."

"Roger that, Marcus."

The Hawk dropped them near the remains of the northern side of the Harbor Bridge. The bright afternoon light glinted off the waters of the harbor. As they jogged toward the park, the ruins of the bridge loomed overhead. Once, it had been an icon of the city, stretching over the harbor like a solid metal coat hanger. The center of the bridge had been blown away, leaving jagged, twisted metal behind.

They rounded the point and the face of Luna Park came into view. The gigantic visage was at least ten meters across, multi-colored, with towers flanking it. It's wide, smiling mouth was the entrance to the park. Somehow, the entire thing had escaped damage during the raptor invasion.

"Bryony was right, it is creepy," Cruz said as they walked through the mouth.

Everything was quiet. No sign of any raptors. Inside, was a wide avenue flanked by colorful buildings made to look like circus tents and castles. It should have been cheery and welcoming, but the park had an eerie, haunted feel. The rides sat silent, and the stalls and restaurants that would have once sold food and drinks were derelict. A large Ferris wheel was visible in the distance ahead, drunkenly tilted to one side.

"The human signatures are in the large building with the yellow-and-white striped roof. It's called the Big Top. It was a function center and concert hall," Elle said.

Santha spotted the large building, with its name emblazoned above the main doors in a circus-style script. Sometime during the last year, the letter B had fallen off.

"Got it," Marcus murmured. "Let's move, Hell Squad."

They entered through the glass doors, Claudia and Gabe going in first.

The foyer contained a large bar, where guests would have grabbed a drink and a bite to eat before a concert. Now, all the bar stools were scattered across the floor like fallen Skittles.

Claudia waved them toward the doors leading into the main auditorium.

"Hell," Marcus muttered.

There were no raptors inside, but what Santha saw made nausea roll through her stomach.

In the huge, open area, there were far more beds than there'd been at the other lab.

Every bed was filled with bodies attached to various machines. At the back of the room, where Santha guessed the stage would be set up, were rows of small cages, stacked two high against the wall. Quiet moaning filled the room.

"Doc?" Marcus said.

Doc Emerson pushed forward. "I'll assess everyone's condition, work out who we can move." She set to work, determination in the set of her jaw. "See if you can find Dr. Lonsdale."

The team spread out. Santha moved down the row of beds, searching the pale faces. At the same time, she went to work, undoing the straps holding some of them to the beds.

"Found him," Gabe called out from the second row of beds.

Santha yanked at a strap that refused to budge.

The woman in the bed had her eyes open, and her mouth gaped. She stared, unseeing, at the ceiling.

"Dammit, come loose," Santha muttered, yanking harder.

"Here." Cruz leaned in from behind and pulled the strap off.

"Thanks." She closed her eyes for a second. "This is…"

"I know." He pressed a warm hand to the nape of her neck. "We'll do what we can to help them."

Santha let her gaze drift over the beds. She already knew a good number of them wouldn't survive, or if they did, they'd never be the same. She didn't need a medical degree to know that some of these people had been broken—physically and mentally.

"Shit. Guys, take a look at this." It was Shaw.

Santha and Cruz hurried over to the back corner, deep in the shadows, where the sniper stood. He had his hands on his hips, his back tense.

"What is it?" Marcus said, striding up.

"Look," Shaw gestured.

Three large tanks stood in a triangular grouping. Three bodies hung in the cloudy liquid inside—two men and one woman, her hair floating like blonde seaweed around her head.

"What the fuck?" Marcus bit out. "Are they alive?"

As Santha neared the tanks, one of the men moved and she jerked back. "I…think so."

She peered through the glass. What the hell were the raptors doing? The man's skin was mottled with dark patches. Then she spied something back behind the tanks and gasped.

"It gets worse." Her stomach turned over. "Look."

A pile of dead bodies lay discarded on the floor behind the tanks. On the top, a man with his chest cracked wide open, and a woman with most of her insides on the outside of her body.

"Shit," Cruz muttered.

"Bastards," Santha spat.

Doc Emerson walked up, her jaw set. "I can't help them all. No matter what I do, even with nano-meds, the damage is too extensive." She shook her head. "What's been done...I've never seen things like this."

"We *can* help them," Marcus said darkly. "We stop their misery." His gaze turned to the tanks. "We won't leave anyone here for those alien fuckers to mess with. Their suffering ends here."

With that, the team went about their gruesome rescue mission. Those who were able to be saved were loaded onto iono-stretchers. Those too far gone were euthanized using the meds Doc Emerson had brought with her.

Marcus assumed the grisly task of draining the tanks and pulling out the three people inside. But as soon as the fluid was gone, the men and the woman died.

"I'm out of drugs, but I think that's everyone," the doctor said, fatigue dragging her shoulders down.

Marcus nodded. "We'll continue to load onto the

stretchers and get them ready for transport.

Cruz was a constant presence by Santha's side. And she was grateful for his quiet strength. This place...it left her feeling scraped raw.

But he was really quiet. "You okay?" she asked.

He shook his head. "No. This is..."

Yeah. There were no words to describe this.

"Cruz?" Marcus called out. "I need a hand over here."

"On it." Cruz touched her shoulder, then jogged over to Marcus.

It was then Santha saw a movement in one of the cages on the back wall. She frowned and peered through the gloom. She'd thought they were empty.

As she neared, a hand reached out between the metal bars. A slim, human hand with long, ragged nails.

Santha peered through the bars and into the thick shadows. "It's okay, we're here to help you."

A harsh growl came from the cage. It sent a rush of goose bumps over Santha's skin. She crouched. "We're going to get you out of there."

"Too...late for me." The rasping voice was hard to understand.

And it was female.

"Let me help," Santha said.

The woman moved, coming closer to the bars.

It took Santha's brain a second to realize what she was looking at. Half the woman's face was mottled with bruises and dark patches where it looked like the skin had died. Her eye was swollen closed.

But the other side of her face was pretty, with bronzed skin and a sad green eye.

A very familiar green eye.

The floor felt as though it had dropped out from under Santha, like the world had suddenly been thrown sideways. Her heart constricted.

No. No. No!

"Kareena?"

***

The anguish in Santha's voice snapped Cruz's head around. He charged toward her. She was standing near the cages at the back of the large room.

Then he saw the woman pressed against the bars.

A woman with the same color eye as Santha.

Oh, fuck. "Santha?"

"It's Kareena. We have to help her." Santha's usually composed face was a mask of horror and pain. "Dr. Emerson!" She yelled the doctor's name. "Please, please help."

Cruz wrapped an arm around Santha, feeling the tension running through her. He waved the doctor over. She came at a jog, holding her scanner.

"Santhy?" The woman shifted in the cage. The raspy voice sounded hesitant, confused. "Is that you?"

"Yes."

The woman shuddered, then she growled at Emerson's approach. "Stay back."

"Kareena, this lady is a doctor, she's here to

help." Santha pulled away from Cruz and crouched down near the cage.

Emerson shot Cruz a worried glance, then looked back at Santha. "You know her?"

Santha's chest shuddered. "She's my sister. Kareena."

Sympathy flickered over the doctor's face. She leaned in closer. "Kareena. This is an m-scanner. I'm going to run it over you, okay?"

Kareena didn't respond but she moved closer to the bars. Santha moaned and Cruz cursed. Kareena had an ugly, ragged row of stitches running from her belly button to her neck.

The scanner lights blinked, then it beeped.

Cruz watched Emerson's face. Saw the way it smoothed into professional blankness. Not a good sign. Not good at all.

She stepped away and nodded at Cruz and Santha to move closer. "I can't make sense of all the scan results. They've...removed most of her organs and replaced them with...I don't know what. Whatever they've done to her...it isn't reversible."

"No," Santha whispered, her eyes wide.

"I don't know what we can do." The doctor sighed. "She's dying."

"There is no living with this." Kareena's growling voice had them all spinning to face her.

Her hands gripped the cage bars. "It burns like acid, like an angry beat inside me." Then her face fell, her eye filled with misery. "It hurts. It's eating me alive." She extended a hand through the cage.

"Help me, Santhy."

Santha instantly grabbed her sister's hand. "I will. I'll get you out and we'll find a way to make it better." Her fingers gripped Kareena's hard.

Kareena made a choking sob. "God, I've missed you."

"I've missed you too." A tear ran down Santha's cheek. "I'm so sorry. If I'd known you were alive…"

"It's okay. Tell me, are you safe? You aren't alone."

"I have been. I've been fighting these alien bastards—"

"Please, I want you to take care of yourself. You were always horrible at that."

Santha gave a hiccupping laugh. "I'm learning. But I've had a little help."

Kareena's eye flicked over Santha's shoulder and landed on Cruz. "Who's he?"

Santha didn't need to look around. "His name is Cruz."

He stepped forward and rested his hands on Santha's shoulders. "I'm hers." He felt her give a slight tremble under his hands.

"Good." Relief flashed in Kareena's green eye. "Good. She needs someone to look after her. She always worked too hard, took on too much." The woman's gaze burned into Cruz. "She'll need you now, more than ever." Her gaze was pleading.

Fuck. He understood what Santha's sister was telling him. *Dammit all to hell.*

"Let me get you out," Santha said.

"No." Kareena's voice turned into a growl again

and her grip on Santha's arm tightened. Her long, jagged nails sliced into Santha's skin.

As Santha hissed in pain, Cruz stepped forward and grabbed Kareena's elbow. He exerted enough pressure that she let go and yanked her arm back inside the cage.

Santha pressed her bleeding arm to her chest, staring at her sister in horror.

"It's too late for me, Santhy."

"No. I've been fighting to avenge your death, now I'll fight to save you. Whatever happens."

Kareena came close to the bars again and sighed. "Listen to me, Santhy. Listen. I want you to pour all that passion and love you have in you into something else. Into him." She nodded in Cruz's direction. "Because the way he looks at you...every woman deserves a man who looks at her that way."

"Kareena—"

"Listen, Santhy. I need your help. One last time."

Santha stiffened. "No—"

"One last time, Santhy-girl. You were always the strong one."

"No." Santha's voice was a strangled whisper. Heedless of the scratches on her arm, she reached for Kareena again, curling her fingers over her sister's on the metal bars.

It cut through Cruz. God, he'd fight any alien, any enemy to save her, but here was one thing he couldn't shield her from.

But he could still take the difficult task away from her.

"I need you," Kareena said quietly. "Please."

Santha was silent for a second. "Cruz, can you wait for me with the others?"

His jaw tightened. "Why don't you let me—?"

"No. Just...if I know you're waiting for me, it'll help."

It was the hardest thing he'd ever had to do. To turn and walk away from her when he knew this was tearing her apart.

He moved over to Marcus and the team. Every step felt like he was walking through mud. His friends were silent, watchful. The rest of the patients waited, loaded on stretchers and ready for evac.

"Cruz, if you or Santha need anything, you just ask," Marcus said.

Cruz nodded. But he knew there was nothing that would make this better for Santha.

Moments later, she walked toward him.

Her face was blank but her eyes were filled with a soul-sucking misery. Her hands were shaking, and one held her knife—still coated in blood.

Chapter Sixteen

Cruz watched Santha walk up to him. The knife clattered to the floor and she threw her arms around him. He pulled her into his chest and she pressed her face into him. She was shaking.

"She thanked me." Santha's hands gripped Cruz's armor. "My baby sister thanked me while I killed her."

"You helped her." Cruz cupped Santha's pale cheeks and forced her to look at him. "She was suffering, Santha. You gave her peace."

"I...want to believe that."

He pressed his forehead to hers. "I'm so sorry, *mi reina*. If I could change this, I would."

"Why bother fighting when we can't save the people we love?" Her harsh words came out on an even harsher whisper.

"Hey." He hated the defeated tone to her voice. "Look around at these other people. We saved them. And...you saved me. From the moment I laid eyes on you, something switched on inside me. Before that, I wasn't sure what I was fighting for."

Her gaze was on his face. "Cruz—"

"You're my fucking reason, Santha. I need you."

The sound of a throat clearing made them both look over.

Marcus stood there. "I'm sorry about your sister."

Santha swallowed. "Thank you."

"I know it's hard, Santha, but I have to ask you to put it aside for now. We need to get these people out of here."

Santha swiped a hand across her face and nodded. "Okay."

Cruz gave her a hard squeeze. "Let's move." The quicker they got back to base the quicker he could help her deal with her grief.

The squad hurried outside, pushing and pulling the stretchers along with them. Marcus had already signaled for Elle to send in the Hawks for the evac.

Cruz felt that itchy feeling he always got when something bad was headed their way. He kept one eye on the rooftops, watching for any sign of raptors.

"Elle, any raptor signatures on screen?" he asked.

"Nothing, Cruz."

That didn't make him feel better. The aliens had to know they'd try and rescue these people. Why just let them waltz in unimpeded?

The itching increased with each second that ticked by. Yeah, something was really off.

Three Hawks rocketed in, landing in a flat area near a half-destroyed roller coaster. They all worked to load the patients into the quadcopters.

They filled the first two copters with patients who were left under the careful attention of members of Emerson's medical team. Only two patients went with Hell Squad and Emerson in the final Hawk.

Soon, the Hawks were motoring back across the city, headed for the base.

"I want the commander dead."

Santha's voice drew Cruz's gaze. She sat hunched in the chair beside him, one hand stroking her crossbow.

"We'll find her. Make her pay."

Santha nodded. But her green eyes were so empty it made Cruz's stomach tight.

She needed time to grieve, but he sure as hell wasn't going to let her do it alone.

He'd give her a reason to live. Even if she didn't want one.

***

Santha stared out the window. The ruined city below just a blur in her vision.

She was trying not to think, not to feel.

But Kareena's face was burned into her brain. Not the smiling, beautiful sister she'd known all her life, but the tortured, beaten face she'd been left with, thanks to the raptors.

God. Santha squeezed her eyes closed. How long would it take until she didn't think about sliding that knife into her sister? Listening to Kareena's quiet words of thanks as Santha had taken her life.

Suddenly alarms blared from the cockpit.

"Fuck," Finn called back. "Strap in Hell Squad, we have two pteros incoming. I'm going to try and pull them off the other two Hawks."

Santha yanked on her harness and beside her Cruz, did the same.

"I knew it was too easy," he grumbled.

The Hawk shuddered and a glance out the side window showed green poison streaking across the sky.

"Missiles incoming," Finn yelled.

The Hawk veered hard right, throwing Santha against Cruz's shoulder hard enough to steal her breath.

She heard him mutter and around them the rest of Hell Squad were cursing and bracing themselves.

The side of the quadcopter imploded, sparks and flames showering them all.

The Hawk fell into a dizzying death spiral. Santha was slammed around, her head striking the side wall.

Her vision dimmed. She heard the roar of the wind, men swearing, alarms blaring.

A sharp, violent burst of pain.

Then nothing.

***

With a groan, Santha opened her eyes. It was dark and a brisk wind ruffled her hair. Beneath her, she felt pavement. And she hurt. She hurt a lot.

She dragged herself up to a sitting position. Pain

stabbed through her right thigh, and she bit her lip to stop from crying out. She glanced down and saw a ragged shard of metal sticking out of her leg. *God.* What had happened?

She looked up and her heart leaped into her throat.

The Hawk lay about fifteen meters away, crashed in the front yard of a house. The copter was barely recognizable—not much more than a twisted lump of metal.

Cruz. Santha tried to stand, but the resulting pain made her stomach revolt. She leaned to the side and retched.

She sank back against what she now realized was a wooden fence. She wasn't going anywhere with this metal in her leg.

After sucking in a few breaths, she gripped the piece of metal. "You can do this, Santha." Quick as she could, without giving it a second thought, she yanked it out.

She panted through the pain, fighting off unconsciousness, her head lolling to the side. Hideous agony flowed through her in a giant wave.

She wasn't sure how long she sat there, but noises made her look up.

Santha squinted and sucked in a shocked breath.

Raptors surrounded the wreck of the Hawk and had lights shining on it.

Her heart hammered in her chest, and she froze in position. No aliens headed in her direction and she exhaled softly. They hadn't noticed her.

Gingerly, she shifted her weight, and pain stabbed through her leg like fire. She bit her lip and forced her scream back down. *Come on, Santha. Get it together.*

She fumbled around at her belt, searching for the med kit, all the while keeping one eye on the raptors crawling all over the Hawk wreckage. She finally managed to get the zipper open and pulled out a bandage, which she clumsily tied around her thigh. She shoved another wad of bandage under it. Dammit, her wound was bleeding a lot. She tried to tell herself she was damn lucky she hadn't hit an artery.

Ahead, she heard guttural shouts and grunts from the raptors as they shifted bits of wreckage and lumps of metal.

And bodies.

No. The thought of Cruz and the other Hell Squad members dead fell on her like a giant weight. No, he couldn't be dead. She couldn't lose him, too.

The raptors dumped two bodies on the ground. Neither were wearing armor. The patients. Neither moved.

Sorrow stabbed at Santha but she pushed it down, hard. She had to focus, and help anyone still alive in the wreck.

Two more raptors shuffled away from the Hawk, carrying a large body between them. They dumped the man on the ground and he groaned. *Marcus.* And he was still alive.

For now.

"Fuck you!" Violent movement from the wreckage caught her attention.

Cruz! She watched three raptors struggling to contain him. Half his face was covered in blood, but the way he was fighting suggested he wasn't injured too badly.

They dumped him near Marcus, and one of the aliens pulled his weapon off his shoulder and aimed it at Cruz.

Terror was like a stone in Santha's throat. She started dragging herself toward them.

She didn't want to die here, in the dirt, and leave the raptors to torture someone else's sister or kill a good man. She would fight until she couldn't fight anymore.

And she didn't want to do it without Cruz by her side. The man had pushed and prodded at her until he was so deep under her skin she knew she'd never get him out. Didn't want to get him out.

She drew her combat knife. It had ended her sister's suffering and now it would take the lives of these alien bastards.

The raptors dragged out more bodies. A swearing Shaw and an unconscious Claudia and Gabe.

"We are going to kill all of you, you bastards," Shaw yelled.

When a raptor nudged Claudia's body with his boot, Shaw kicked at him. "Get the fuck away from her."

Cruz was sitting, watching the raptors around them. Even from a distance, Santha could see his powerful body coiling.

Her pulse jumped. *No, you hero, just wait for me.*

But he launched himself at them, striking like a viper. He'd stabbed two before the rest were on him.

Raptors were punching and kicking him, pummeling his body.

Marcus and Shaw moved to help, but they were outnumbered, and quickly subdued.

Santha pushed to her feet, gripping the fence to help her stand. Her leg screamed in pain and couldn't take much weight. The exoskeleton in her armor took a lot of her weight, so she knew the injury was bad. She drew her crossbow.

She started forward, her right leg dragging in the dirt. She aimed at the biggest raptor beating Cruz and fired.

She was already aiming at the second before the first dropped.

The other raptors swiveled, spotted her. They left a groaning Cruz and ran at her, lifting their weapons. Pushing through her pain, she sank low and stabbed at the nearest raptors, cutting through the weak spots in their armor. Two more stumbled backward.

The rest were almost on her when Cruz appeared from the darkness. He yanked a gun from the nearest raptor body, aimed, and unloaded their own poison into them.

Shaw appeared and pummeled another raptor with his fists. Marcus emerged from the shadows, still looking dazed, but he took down another with brutal kicks.

Before long, all the raptors were down.

The men stood there, breathing heavily. Santha felt a wave of dizziness, but she only had eyes for Cruz.

He was alive. That was all that mattered.

Two pteros flashed overhead, shining blinding lights down on them.

"We need to get into shelter," Marcus yelled.

Shaw scooped up Claudia, and Marcus heaved Gabe over his shoulder.

Cruz wrapped an arm around Santha, helping her hobble forward. "What about the others? Reed, Finn, the doc?"

Marcus' jaw tightened. "We'll—"

Raptor fire cut through the night.

"Go!" Marcus shouted. "We'll come back for them."

Together, they reached the ruined shell of a two-story house that looked like it had once been a comfortable family home. As they crashed through the front door, Santha caught a glimpse of photos hanging askew on the walls. Parents smiling, hands on the shoulders of two teenaged boys. She wondered if any of them had survived.

"In here." Marcus shouldered his way into the kitchen. "The appliances will give us more protection from any weapons' fire."

"Shit, you're bleeding." Cruz helped Santha down to the floor and she leaned against the wall.

He gripped her thigh, his big hands gentle. "This is bad."

"I've had worse."

His face looked beyond grim, and coated in blood, his sexy good looks were hidden. Now he simply looked scary, like something from a horror movie. Funny that her heart still beat extra hard just looking at him. He was alive and that was all she cared about.

As he studied her wound, he pressed down on the wadded fabric.

"Ow!"

"It's still bleeding." His other hand cupped her cheek. "When I came to and couldn't find you…"

She put her hand over his. "I'm okay. I got thrown clear of the wreckage."

It was only then that Santha became aware of a tinny voice screeching at her. She frowned, confused. Where was the sound coming from? Then, she realized her earpiece had been damaged, but that Elle's voice was still just barely getting through.

The woman sounded frantic.

Santha touched her ear. "Elle?"

***

Cruz watched Marcus' head whip around.

"The raptors took our earpieces," Marcus growled.

Santha pulled hers out and handed it over.

Hell Squad's leader shoved it in his ear. "Elle? Baby?"

The big man was silent for a moment and Cruz watched him close his eyes for a second.

"I'm okay. We made it out of the crash. We're holed up." Pause. "I know. I know. Calm down."

Cruz couldn't believe they'd made it. He'd been so worried about finding Santha he'd barely thought of anything else. Then she'd come out of the darkness, raining crossbow bolts like an avenging warrior queen.

His queen.

He placed a med-patch over her wound. The cut was jagged and ugly, but the bleeding was finally slowing. He finished redoing her bandage.

"I'm going to give you a shot. It's only mild, but it'll take the edge off the pain."

She nodded. "I won't say no." He pressed the injector to her thigh.

"Okay, Elle, I got it," Marcus said. "We'll hang on until help arrives, I want...Elle? Elle?" He slammed a fist into the wall. "Raptors jammed the signal."

"What'd she say?" Cruz asked.

"Help's on the way. But with all the pteros in the air, and the increased raptor presence, they can't send Hawks."

"They're coming via the ground?" Shaw sat back, his head thunking against the wall. "That'll take at least an hour." He cast a worried glance down at Claudia. She lay on her side, her head resting on his thigh. She hadn't regained consciousness.

"She's hurt bad."

"We'll get her back to base." Cruz hid his own worry. "She's tough."

Gabe groaned and slowly came to. "What the hell?"

"Hey, how are you feeling?" Marcus crouched down near the other man. "Took a bad knock to the head."

Gabe rubbed his temple. "Fuck. Feels like I was on an all-night bender."

Marcus studied the man's eyes. "You'll hold until we get back."

"Yeah." Then Gabe looked around, taking in their surroundings, and stiffened. "Where's the doc? Where's Emerson?"

The team all traded glances.

Gabe pushed to his feet, swayed and grabbed the wall to stay upright. "Where the fuck is she?"

"No one saw her," Marcus said. "Finn and Reed are missing too. They might still be in the wreck."

He didn't say the words, but Cruz knew everyone was wondering if there were only bodies to recover.

Something wild flashed in Gabe's eyes. Something Cruz had never seen before in the contained, intense man.

"I'm going to look for her—" He made a move toward the hall.

Marcus blocked his path. "Stand down, Gabe. You go out there, you're just committing suicide."

"We'll find her." Cruz caught Gabe's dark gaze. "And Reed and Finn. You have to survive in order to find her."

Gabe's mouth twisted but he nodded. "The patients?"

"Dead," Santha said quietly. "I saw the raptors drag their bodies out."

The team was quiet.

Gabe moved toward the window. "Fuck. Marcus, alien reinforcements have arrived."

Hell Squad crowded near the window. Raptor vehicles were pulling up and raptors filled the street. Overhead, pteros circled like hungry birds.

"We need to move." Gabe's voice was urgent as he swiveled.

Cruz frowned. He didn't see anything to warrant the urgency. But he knew Gabe had enhanced abilities from his time in a secret military experiment. Not that he ever talked about it.

"What? What did you see?" Marcus asked.

"Back in the shadows, they're setting up mortars." Gabe's face looked lethal. "They're going to blow us out of here."

Chapter Seventeen

"Everyone up, we have to go," Marcus shouted.

Cruz cursed under his breath and helped Santha up. He saw the pain reflected in her eyes. She was biting her lip hard enough it was bleeding.

"The pain's still bad?"

"I can handle it." She tossed her head back. "Let's go."

Marcus headed over to Shaw and Claudia. "I'll carry her."

"I've got her," Shaw said.

"I need you on a gun."

Shaw nodded reluctantly, and took hold of the carbine Marcus had managed to grab.

They were about to head out the back door when it slammed open. Shaw sprung forward, gun up.

Reed shouldered through the opening, one arm around a limping Finn, whose head and face were covered with blood. He was clutching his left arm to his chest.

"Thank fuck. You guys okay?" Marcus asked.

Reed nodded. "A few cuts and bruises. Finn here has a broken arm."

"But my legs are working fine," the pilot muttered.

"Emerson? Either of you see Emerson?" Gabe asked.

The two men shook their heads. Reed cursed. "I assumed she was with you guys."

"We have to go." Marcus motioned to the door. "We're about to get a few mortars in here."

"Shit." Reed headed back out the door. "We came the long way so I know a way out. Stick to the buildings and trees because the pteros are lighting up the place." He pointed. "This yard backs onto an alley. We cross the alley, then go through the adjacent house. It backs onto some parkland. There's a river with an intact footbridge, which is too narrow for vehicles."

"So any raptors would have to pursue on foot." Marcus nodded. "Good."

"The river isn't too deep, so they could cross it in vehicles. But it'll slow them down."

They headed off. Cruz did his best to take as much of Santha's weight as he could, but her harsh gasps and the small hitches in her breath told him she was in agony.

They raced from tree to tree in the backyard, pausing when a ptero flashed a floodlight on the lawn. Once darkness fell again, they all sprinted to the back fence.

Cruz pushed through the gate, across the alley, and then followed the others into another abandoned house. This one had not survived unscathed. The roof in the living room had caved in, and all the walls had large cracks running through them.

They were all in the hall when an explosion hit.

Cruz swiveled and through the shattered front windows, saw the first house they'd sheltered in had been hit by a mortar. Crimson flames rose into the night sky.

"Keep moving," Marcus said.

Another explosion, this one big enough to shake the floor beneath them.

"They aren't messing around," Santha murmured.

Hell Squad hurried through the darkened house and out the back door. They crossed the tiny yard, trampling overgrown flower beds, and spilled out into a small parkland.

The river glimmered ahead under the moonlight.

It was a good fifty meters away.

Across empty field.

Cruz tightened his hold on Santha. "No cover."

A ptero whizzed past overhead, its light swinging in a crisscrossing search pattern.

"We don't have a better option." Marcus looked back as another explosion rocked the night.

Reed pointed a little to the left. "The bridge is that way."

"No point hanging around back here." Shaw lifted his gun. "Go. I'll bring up the rear and pick off any raptors that head our way."

Marcus shifted Claudia's weight and nodded. "No risks though. You follow as soon as we get close to the bridge."

"You got it, boss." His gaze drifted over Claudia's face. "You just focus on getting everyone out of here."

"Don't play the hero, Shaw. Everyone prefers you as the playboy."

"Fuck you, Marcus."

Marcus gave him a tight smile then turned toward the field. "Let's go."

The grass was long enough to hamper them, tangling around their knees, slowing their pace. Cruz scanned the area, watching for any movement. He decided not to mention the possibility of a velox prowling around. They had enough to worry about.

"There's the bridge," Santha said.

The sound of weapons fire screamed through the night.

"Faster," Marcus yelled.

Reed and Finn reached the bridge first, followed by Gabe. Gabe swiveled and lifted his weapon. He crouched at the edge to cover them.

Marcus crossed over, Claudia now slung over his shoulder. Cruz helped Santha hobble over the gentle arch of the bridge.

Cruz glanced over his shoulder, saw Shaw sprinting across the field. Behind him, a sea of raptors was racing toward them.

"Fuck. Marcus!"

Cruz heard his friend swearing.

Then three pteros screamed overhead.

Cruz urged Santha on. Lights swung onto the bridge, turning night into day.

Then the world went up in flames.

***

Gabe

Gabe came to with the top half of his body hanging over the bridge. His ears were ringing and the headache from hell was beating inside his skull like a jackhammer.

He turned his head and saw the dark waters below steadily streaming by, oblivious to the life-and-death fight raging above. *Shit.*

With a groan, he sat up. Then he heard a deep moan from nearby.

Cruz and Santha were tangled together a couple of meters away. He saw Santha trying to push Cruz's dead weight off her.

In a crouch, Gabe made his way over to them. Damn, a chunk of the bridge had been blown away when the ptero had fired on them. There was just a narrow walkway left to the other side.

Santha had managed to get Cruz off her and was on her knees by his side, his face cupped in her hands.

"Cruz? Cruz, can you hear me?"

Gabe kneeled. Jesus, Cruz was bleeding heavily from his side. Some of his armor had been ripped off in the blast. "He okay?"

"I don't know." She tapped his cheek, none too gently. "Cruz, dammit, I need you to live. You aren't going to die on me now."

He groaned again but didn't open his eyes.

Shouts made Gabe and Santha look up.

Shaw had made it to the bridge and was hunkered down shooting. Gabe's jaw tightened. Raptors were heading their way.

Dammit, he needed to go and help Shaw. Turning his head, he saw Marcus helping Reed with Claudia and Finn on the far side of the bridge.

"Come on, I'll carry Cruz to the other side." Gabe grabbed his teammate and heaved him onto his shoulder.

Santha ran a hand over Cruz's hair in a quick caress. "Be okay. I'm going to make sure you get out of here."

Something in that small gesture made Gabe's chest hurt. It was so...intimate. He knew Cruz was completely gone over Santha, but it looked like it was more than just sex for both of them.

He cast a quick glance in the direction of the raptors and thought of Emerson. Where was she? His heart was a hard hammer against his ribs. Was she even still alive?

Whatever happened, he sure as hell wasn't leaving here without her.

"Gabe?"

With a shake of his head, he nodded at Santha. Together, they walked carefully across the narrow strip left in the middle of the bridge and then hurried over to Marcus.

"Cruz is hurt," Santha said.

"Put him down here," Marcus said.

"I need to go and help Shaw." Gabe studied the trees beyond the bridge. "That area of heavy trees looks like the best option for some shelter."

Marcus nodded, but his blue eyes were grim. They both knew that holding on until help arrived was going to be tough.

Santha cast one more look at Cruz, then faced Gabe. "I'm coming to help you."

Damn, he liked her.

They wasted no time joining Shaw. They both kneeled and started firing.

"Nice shooting, *mi reina*," Shaw said. He had a burn on his face which made him look like a horror movie extra.

"Only Cruz calls me that." She sighted the nearest raptor and took him down.

"And Cruz will kick your ass if he hears you calling her that," Gabe added.

They kept firing, but more and more raptors kept coming.

But strangely enough, most kept back from the bridge and didn't engage. They were forming a perimeter.

"What the fuck are you waiting for?" Shaw goaded. "Pussies!"

Gabe kept shooting. This wasn't just about their survival anymore. It was about the survival of everything human.

And it was about Emerson.

Gabe clamped down on the rioting mass of conflicting emotions inside him.

Three raptor vehicles growled into view, roaring over the grass. They pulled up behind the line of raptor soldiers.

Gabe stopped shooting. Santha lowered her pistols. Shaw kept his carbine aimed but also stopped firing.

"What now?" Gabe muttered.

A tall lean raptor stepped out of the lead vehicle. Santha stiffened. "The commander."

Gabe felt the tension radiating off Santha. They all watched as the alien leader reached the head of the line of raptors.

"I…have something…of yours." The commander's English was slow and halting, but it was easy enough to understand.

Another raptor pushed forward, nudging something ahead of him.

Emerson was forced onto her knees in front of the commander.

All the air rushed out of Gabe's lungs at the sight. Her head hung to her chest, her arms by her side, hands resting in the dirt. Every inch of her was covered in blood.

Gabe made a choking noise and surged to his feet. He was taking a step when hands grabbed his arms. Hard.

"Damn, you're a strong bastard," Shaw grumbled.

"You can't help her if you're dead," Santha snapped.

Gabe stilled, but he didn't pull his gaze off the woman on her knees in the dirt.

"Think it through, mate," Shaw said quietly. "Let's play this out. It's our best chance of helping the doc."

Gabe felt like he was going to snap. But fuck it all, they were right. He had to save her and he couldn't do that if he was dead.

Finally, he nodded and sank back into a crouch. But he continued to scan the aliens around Emerson, waiting for the right moment to free her.

Using his enhanced senses, he picked up Emerson's breathing. It was a little fast. Her heartbeat was fast as well. She was terrified.

"I want to talk." The commander stared at them. "One of you...must come to me."

Not good. Gabe fisted his hand. But it'd get him closer to Emerson. "I'll do it."

Shaw snorted. "Mate, I don't trust your usually solid control. You're like a Backfire explosive waiting to detonate."

Santha drew in a trembling breath. "I'll go."

"No."

Cruz's voice. Gabe looked up and saw the man sink down beside Santha.

"You shouldn't even be upright," she said.

"Got to make sure you stay alive."

Gabe watched her face, saw it soften.

"I don't have a death wish, Cruz. Someone has to go out there."

"I want...to talk to the...female," the commander said.

Santha released a long breath. "Well, decision made."

"It's a trap," Cruz gripped her arm.

"We'll all die the instant they open fire." She placed her hand over his and then pressed a quick kiss to his lips. "Let's see what she's got to say."

He gave a reluctant nod.

Gabe didn't envy the man watching his woman walk into danger.

He looked back at Emerson, willed her to look up, acknowledge them, anything. But she stayed in the hunched-over position, beaten.

What the hell had they done to her?

Santha lifted her head and walked forward. Gabe could see from the way she held herself she was in pain, but her chin stayed high. Cruz had chosen well.

But then he focused back on the doctor who'd become his beacon in the dark. From the moment he'd lost his brother, Emerson had been the only thing that had eased his pain.

I'm coming for you, Doc. I'm coming.

Chapter Eighteen

Santha's left leg raged with pain, but the rest of her hurt almost as much. She was just a massive ball of aches. She didn't rush toward the commander. One, she didn't want the alien bitch to think she was jumping to obey her orders. And two, Santha probably couldn't if she wanted to—her leg would give out on her.

She felt the slow slide of blood soaking into her underclothes. The rush to escape and the fighting had set her wound bleeding again. She wouldn't last too much longer before she passed out.

She kept her gaze on the commander and all those horrible, raging emotions rose up. Kareena's features flashed before Santha's eyes. Here was the face of this alien invasion. The one person Santha wanted to kill more than she wanted anything.

Santha came to a halt a few meters away. "Emerson, you okay?"

The doctor didn't say anything. Damn. What had they done to her?

Santha pinned a glare on the alien commander. "Just so you know, I'm going to kill you. I don't care if it's fast or slow. I just want you dead."

"Another will replace me." It was a guttural snarl.

"I don't care. It was you who had my sister dragged away, you tortured her in your freak show lab and took her away from me. I'll make you pay for that. You understand?"

There was nothing warm about the commander's red gaze. "Your emotions make you weak. We are here to teach you strength, to make your species stronger."

Santha blinked. What? They wanted humans to *join* them?

"Your species is feeble. Ruled by useless emotions, you lack—" she seemed to search for the right word "—focus. A single driving goal. From our study of you, your species is fragmented across your planet, fighting amongst yourselves."

"We're individuals. We each can choose who we are and what we do."

The alien made a throaty noise. "Your emotions made you an easy target. But we will help make you strong."

Santha felt a shiver up her spine. "What, so we become killers like you?"

"Not killers—fighters. Resilient."

Was strength the only thing these aliens valued? "There's more to life than war and fighting. We aren't cold like you. You'll never understand us and we'll *never* join you."

The commander watched Santha like she was a worthless bug. She shrugged. "You do not have a choice."

"We'll fight you. Every step of the way."

"Even if it means your death?"

"Yep." Santha tightened her grip on the knife. *I love you, Cruz.*

She launched herself at the commander.

It was the element of surprise, and the added strength from her exoskeleton, that helped Santha take the alien down to the ground.

But the commander was still bigger and stronger. They rolled across the grass, Santha trying to force her knife toward the alien's throat.

The commander fended her off, looked back at her troops and snarled something in her language. The closest raptors, those hovering nearby, snarled in reply but withdrew.

Then Santha saw gunfire light up the night, but when the commander elbowed her in the face, she reminded herself that she couldn't worry about the other raptors.

Because the one fighting her was deadly enough.

She managed to get a good cut across the commander's face. The raptor bared her teeth.

They rolled again. The commander ended up on top. Her large hands wrapped around Santha's neck.

Santha smacked at her with a fist and then changed her grip on the knife and plunged it though a gap in the alien's armor under her arm.

With a cry, the commander reared back and let go.

Santha coughed and dragged in air. She rolled and leaped to her feet.

Then Cruz was there, landing a vicious kick that sent the commander stumbling.

Santha stood. Air was heaving in and out of her lungs. Pain was an ugly, living thing that invaded every cell. But all she had to do was think of her sister and Santha's resolve hardened. Then she glanced again at the man standing beside her.

She was fighting for so much more than revenge. Pain was nothing compared to that.

She limped forward, her right foot now dragging in the dirt. The commander rose, a good foot taller than Santha.

But the alien wasn't fueled by righteous anger, or painful grief...or by hope, all of it needing an outlet. Those emotions the commander thought were weak gave Santha an edge.

The commander circled Santha and pulled a jagged blade from her belt. When her nearby raptor soldiers inched closer, she yelled at them again.

They instantly stepped back.

Santha pulled her combat knife and matched the alien's movements. Cruz was a solid, supportive presence behind her.

Then the commander jumped forward. Santha met her.

Santha ducked and dodged the creature's swipes. She used her own blade to cut and slice. One after another, tiny little cuts here and there, where there were gaps, or where the commander had no armor.

Some didn't penetrate the alien's thick scales.

But some did. And they bled.

As they fought, Santha could see the commander was weakening.

"This is how we'll defeat you," Santha said. "One small cut at a time. Each one will leave you bleeding."

The commander spat a mouthful of blood onto the ground. "You are nothing compared to the might of the Gizzida."

"We'll keep coming." Santha snuck in low and cut the commander above her boot. "We'll never stop. No matter what you do to us."

Limping, the commander lunged, a sloppy strike. Santha opened up a large gash in the alien's arm.

"We'll weaken you," Santha continued. "We'll keep fighting. Humans, we're stubborn like that. You said we lacked focus, but you've given us a big one..." Santha landed a side kick hard in the commander's stomach. As the alien stumbled, Santha followed it with a quick slash to the neck. "Survival."

The alien leader pulled back, but the tip of the knife kissed across the more delicate skin of her throat. She swiped at the blood and opened her mouth in what Santha guessed was a smile.

"Once, I was like you. But they made me stronger. I see good skills in you. You would make a good leader, too."

"Never." Santha leaped up and slammed her knife into the back of the commander's shoulder. She leaped away before the alien could grab her.

"We will absorb your species and everything you

have of value. There is nothing you can do to stop us."

A sick feeling knocked through Santha. "No." Grim determination rose up. "We'll stop you. We'll fight and we'll never stop fighting."

"You cannot defeat us!" The commander charged like a bull.

She slammed into Santha and they hit the dirt. The alien was tearing at Santha, using her claws to scratch and gouge.

"Yes, we can. You'll make mistakes." Santha jammed the knife into the commander's throat. "Like fighting me and thinking I was beneath you. And that's when we'll win."

The commander's overlarge eyes bulged. Blood gushed over both of them. She made a gurgling sound.

"We'll show you just what humanity is made of." Santha leaned up, heedless of the alien blood all over her, and twisted the knife. "That's for my sister, you bitch."

When the commander flopped forward, with a final, gurgling breath, Santha heaved her off.

And then Cruz was there, pulling her up.

A deep, guttural cry raced through the raptors lined up in front of them.

Fuck. Santha gripped Cruz. She might have killed the commander but there was no way they could fight all of these raptors.

"Cruz?"

"Yes, *mi reina*?"

"I...I..." There was so much she wanted to say.

And so much she still wanted to do. "I wouldn't have picked anyone else to die with."

He yanked her off her feet and kissed her.

She absorbed the taste of him, her hands tangling in his hair. She waited for the hail of raptor fire to hit them.

Suddenly, the sounds of gunning engines filled the night. Bright lights streamed around them. The raptors cried out and started running, confused and leaderless.

Santha and Cruz turned.

Armored Z6-Hunter vehicles roared across the river, the armor plating keeping water out of the engines as it flowed across the vehicles' hoods. Then, the Hunters charged into the field, autocannons firing.

"Squad Nine has damn good timing. Again." Cruz started pulling her back toward the bridge. "I owe Roth a drink. Or seven."

The battled raged around them, but ahead on the ruins of the bridge, she saw Marcus waving them over. Beside him, Gabe was cradling a sobbing Emerson.

"Cruz?"

"Yeah?"

"I think I'm going to pass out now."

Blackness swallowed Santha, but she knew Cruz would catch her.

***

Santha woke and lay still on the bed. The room was dark and the sheets smelled like Cruz.

She sat up, dragging a hand through her tangled hair. She was naked, the cool air raising goose bumps on her skin. Her healed skin. As she drew the sheet up, she noted that not a single scratch marred her body. Her thigh looked fine. Even the scar she had from where Kareena had pushed her out of a tree when she was seven was gone.

"How do you feel?"

Santha started. Dammit, she hadn't even known he was in the room. Glancing over, she saw the outline of him in the armchair. "I feel pretty good, considering. So we either got out okay or my afterlife looks like it's going to involve a whole lot of hot sex in an underground base."

Cruz stood, walked over and planted his hands either side of her on the bed. "You promised you wouldn't get yourself killed."

Okay, there was more than a bit of a dangerous edge in his voice. "And here I am, hale and hearty."

He moved so fast, she let out a squeak. He grabbed her upper arms and yanked her up until their noses brushed. "Barely. I had to fucking pump your heart every minute of that drive back to base. They had to revive you, then they pumped you full of nano-meds."

Oh, her poor man. She got her hands on his chest. "I'm sorry, Cruz. But I'm alive. You're alive." A thought rushed through her. "The commander?"

"Dead."

Santha felt something unfurl inside her. A

release of that tight, hot, nasty ball that had been lodged inside her for over a year. She stared into Cruz's handsome face. Kareena wouldn't get to live the life she'd deserved. But in that cage where she'd died, Kareena had made Santha promise that she'd live for both of them.

Santha gave Cruz a hard shove. He fell back on the bunk, his lean body sprawled out. She crawled up on top of him.

"I need some proof this is real and not some injury-induced daydream," she said.

He raised an eyebrow. "Really?"

"Yep." She leaned down and nipped at his lips. Hmm, he tasted so good. Their tongues tangled, his hands cupping her shoulders.

Then she pulled away from his too-tempting mouth and dragged her lips over his stubbled jaw, down the line of his strong throat. She bit the spot where his neck met his shoulder and enjoyed his groan.

She kept going. Tracing every inch of his hard chest with her tongue. She scraped his nipples with teeth and nails and he arched up into her. She trailed her mouth over the unreal sculpted ridges of his stomach. Every bit of this strength and power was all hers.

She moved lower. He moaned her name. She cupped his thick, heavy cock in her hands. Then without warning him, she sucked the mushroom head of it into her mouth.

"*Mi reina*...so damn good." His hands clenched in her hair.

She sucked more of him in, as far as she could go. She bobbed up and down, giving him all the pleasure she could. His body was tense as a board beneath her. God, could anything make a woman feel more powerful than having a strong man completely at her mercy?

"Enough."

He pulled her back and reared up. Before she could react, he flipped her onto her back and his heavy weight sank down on top of her.

He grabbed her hands and slammed them above her head. Then his cock nudged between her legs and he thrust home.

She cried out, said his name over and over. She jerked against his hold but he held her down, his hips pistoning as he plunged into her.

Santha felt every inch of her body tightening. His possession was so hot, so all consuming. She was his and he was hers. She knew right now he was working out his desire and his fear. And she loved every minute of it.

"Cruz, I'm going to come."

"Go over, *mi reina*. Let me feel you squeezing my cock, milking me hard."

His dirty talk had her tipping over the edge. Her mind blanked and her orgasm crashed over her like a wave.

When she opened her eyes, he was still looming over her, thrusting inside her. His dark gaze locked on hers.

"I'm in love with you, Santha."

A bright burst of warmth lit up her insides.

"Good." Her voice cracked. "That's good, soldier, because the feeling's mutual."

He shifted the angle of his hips and she felt him brushing against her swollen clit with each stroke. It didn't take long for the electric sensations to grow again.

"That's it," he murmured, savage satisfaction in his tone. "Come again, *mi amor*. Let's come together."

She threw her head back and his name ripped from her throat. A second later, his thrusts got faster, harder and he poured himself inside her.

***

Cruz watched Santha eating the fresh fruit he'd brought for her and felt a massive flood of satisfaction. She was alive, she was here, and she was his.

She loved him. Man, if that didn't just blow his mind, he didn't know what would.

She stopped chewing and it was clear she was lost in thought. "So, I guess I'm moving in."

No way was he letting her go back to the city. "Yes."

"We'll have to eat in the dining room, though. Or you'll have to cook."

He smiled. "Deal."

She leaned back. "And I expect you to play the guitar for me at least a couple of times a week." She grinned. "A private performance."

He ran his tongue over his teeth. "Only if you

dance for me…and touch yourself."

She slapped his shoulder. Then her face turned serious. "I can't just sit in here, in the bowels of this base every day." She looked him. "I'll go crazy."

He felt his jaw tighten. He'd known this was coming. "You want to join the squad?"

Her eyebrows went up. "And drive Marcus crazy by not following his commands all the time?"

Cruz's lips quirked. "Yeah." He knew he'd go crazy knowing she was out on a squad, fighting raptors. But, he was a member of Hell Squad and she'd have to deal with him going out, so he couldn't exactly demand she stay here, safe and protected.

All he could do was be here for her when she got back and keep showing her all the good things life had to offer.

"You'd be okay with me joining a squad?" she asked, watching him carefully.

"No." He'd give her honesty. "But I'll support whatever you want to do."

She smiled. "You are one of the good guys, Cruz Ramos. I have to say, I'm not crazy about knowing you'll be out there risking yourself day after day." She scraped a nail down his cheek. "But humanity needs its warriors, its heroes. And I'll have to do my bit to make sure my hero stays as safe as possible." She straightened. "You know I work better alone. And I was thinking the base's reconnaissance needs beefing up. The drones are great, but they can't give you the same intel you can get from the ground. I'd like to see about creating a team of reconnaissance officers. Who go in quietly, gather intel, and come home without being seen."

Cruz let out the breath that had been lodged in his chest. It was still dangerous, but it was what she was good at. And much safer than landing in the middle of a firefight. "I think Holmes will be beside himself to have you." Cruz stood and nabbed her hand. "Come on, I have something for you."

He led her through the tunnels. At one intersection they met Marcus and Elle strolling with Reed and Roth.

"Santha, you look much better." Elle grabbed her hand and smiled.

"Thanks," Santha said, squeezing the other woman's hand in return. She glanced over at Roth. "And thanks for the timely rescue."

The man nodded. "Just sorry we didn't get there a bit sooner."

She frowned. "Everyone made it out okay, right?" She looked up at Cruz. "Claudia?"

"Is fine. Shaw is in the infirmary with her, bugging her to death." Cruz swallowed his frustration. "It's Gabe we're worried about."

"Emerson's taking some time to recover. She was badly beaten and she's suffering flashbacks and nightmares," Marcus said. "Gabe's taking it badly."

Gabe clearly felt protective of the doctor and this, on top of his brother's death, was weighing hard on him. But Cruz didn't know what else he could do to help his teammate.

"We're headed topside," Cruz said.

Marcus nodded, slinging an arm around Elle. "We're headed to the dining room. Join us later?"

Cruz waved as he pulled Santha along.

"We'll take Bryony with us to the dining room," he said. "She's been cleared to leave the infirmary for short periods."

Santha smiled. "She has? That's great. I want to get some clothes for her. Something that's hers."

"One step ahead of you. I used my clothing credits and got her a few things." He felt heat in his cheeks. "Elle helped."

"Cruz Ramos picking out clothes for a little girl?" Santha didn't even try and hide her smile. "She'll love them."

He shrugged one shoulder. "I've seen a lot kids who didn't make it. Before the aliens came—" he thought of his cousins' victims "—and after. I want to see her thrive."

Santha's hand tightened on his arm. "I couldn't save Kareena, but together we'll do everything we can to help Bryony."

They exited the base through a tunnel and ladder, and stepped out into the sunlight. The gentle slope of the hill was covered in thick grass and a riot of wildflowers.

"God, it's beautiful." Santha breathed deep. "Things like this give me hope that we can take back our planet and drive those murdering bastards away."

"We will. The local raptor forces are scrambling since losing the commander. We just have to keep slicing."

She blushed. "Ah, my little speech."

"It was motivating as hell."

She turned back to the meadow. "We'll beat them. We won't give up. We owe it to the people we've lost."

He slid an arm over her shoulders and led her to the tree line. "Look."

There were two simple markers set into the ground. The first had the name Ezekiel "Zeke" Jackson inscribed on it. The second marker was a simple carved piece of wood. On it, Cruz had carved Kareena's name, beloved sister of Santha.

Santha stared at the simple marker and pressed a fist to her mouth.

Cruz shifted uncomfortably. "Are those tears in your eyes?"

"Yes. But good ones." She pressed her face against his chest. "Thank you. It's beautiful and I love it. I have no idea what I did to deserve you."

"I feel the same way about you. But I'll spend every day making sure I deserve you."

Her arms slipped around him. "Just spend every day loving me. That's enough."

Only a few weeks before, he'd been running on empty, had thought there was nothing else left for him. Nothing else to live for.

Now, he had hope and love bursting through him.

And so much to live for.

Santha lifted her face up to him, the sunshine lighting up her features. "Now, kiss me, soldier."

Cruz smiled. "Yes, ma'am."

I hope you enjoyed Santha and Cruz's story.

Hell Squad continues with GABE, the story of sexy, brooding Gabe and smart, stubborn doctor, Emerson. Read on for a preview of the first chapter.

Don't miss out! For updates about new releases, action romance info, free books, and other fun stuff, sign up for my VIP mailing list and get your free copy of the Phoenix Adventures novella, *On a Cyborg Planet.*

Visit here to get started:
www.annahackettbooks.com

FREE DOWNLOAD

JOIN THE ACTION-PACKED ADVENTURE!

Formats: Kindle, ePub, PDF

Read the first chapter of Gabe

"We're losing him!"

Dr. Emerson Green ignored her nurse's cry, gritted her teeth and kept working. Her gloved hands and arms were covered in blood up to her elbows, as she focused on saving the man on her operating table. "More blood."

Norah Daniels, the most reliable nurse on Emerson's team, worked to pump blood into their patient.

Emerson stared up at the glowing screen of the high-tech monitor attached to the man. It was one of only two that had survived the alien invasion and she was grateful they had it.

"Come on," she urged. He wasn't responding. He was bleeding somewhere, but she couldn't damn well find it.

"Max, can you isolate any sources of bleeding?"

The surgical robot beside her moved one of its four slender arms. "Negative, Dr. Green," the robot's modulated voice intoned. "The extent of the foreign damage is hampering my abilities."

Emerson leaned over the patient's open belly. She stared at the ugly damage the aliens had done to him—cutting him open, burning, scoring—carrying out their obscene tests. She had no idea what the aliens were trying to accomplish in their horror labs, but the patients the human commando teams had managed to rescue all had hideous injuries they'd have to deal with for the rest of their lives.

Not to mention the nightmares.

Emerson had tried to put them back together, to heal them. But some of them would always have scars—visible or not.

Her safety glasses fogged and she cursed under her breath. "New glasses."

Another nurse hurried to change out Emerson's glasses. There was some problem with the base ventilation. She knew the tech team was working on fixing it, but these things took time. Keeping a hidden underground base full of survivors running was a full-time job and their solar-power system was overloaded on most days.

"His pulse is dropping."

Dammit. There was too much blood. The extensive scarring and fresh injuries were hiding the problem, and no matter how much she searched, she couldn't find it. The muscles across her shoulders were stretched to breaking point. "Give him a shot of noxapin. A hundred mil."

When Norah didn't obey, Emerson looked up. "What's wrong? Come on."

The woman's round, dark-skinned face was tense. "We're almost out."

Noxapin was a highly experimental drug that hadn't finished trials before the aliens had invaded. But it had been magic at keeping people alive long enough to survive surgery. Emerson had counted herself lucky that the medical supplies they'd scavenged had included it.

But they were almost through their stores, and clearly no one else believed this man was going to make it.

"Give it to him." She wasn't damn well giving up. On anyone.

They kept working. Emerson worked around Max as the robot's arms, with their different attachments, helped her. Emerson was in charge of the base's medical teams, it was her responsibility to do everything she could to help and heal anyone who was sick or injured. She mightn't be out on the front line, fighting the dinosaur-like raptors, but this was her way of fighting. Sewing people back together, saving their lives, pumping them full of nano-meds when their bodies were too injured to heal themselves.

Except whatever the aliens had done to this man had changed him so much that the tiny medical robots, that could heal a person in just hours, had stopped from working.

But she refused to give up. She'd been treating wounds and putting people back together ever since she'd first seen the huge alien ship blotting out the night sky over Sydney. Images flashed behind her eyes. She and her colleagues at the North Sydney Private Hospital had run up to the roof as soon as the ship had been spotted. An ugly, almost animal-looking thing.

Emerson had had a prime view when the small raptor ptero ships had poured out of the mothership and rained down on the unsuspecting humans below.

Most of whom had died.

Well, she damn well wasn't losing this one. She kept working, clamping, cauterizing, cutting out damaged tissue. She barked out orders for the surgical robot, for equipment, blood, more drugs.

"Emerson? Emerson?"

With aching tiredness dragging down on her, she looked over at Norah.

"He's gone, sweetie."

That's when Emerson's brain registered the constant shrill tone of the monitor.

She looked down. The man's face was relaxed, his skin pale. A dramatic contrast to the bright red of his blood all over her hands.

Sorrow dug into her like a burrowing worm. It knew just where to head to inflict maximum pain. "Time of death, 5:35 pm." She deactivated Max, the robot's arms slowly lowering. She stepped away from the table.

Another life she hadn't been able to help. She let herself feel the full punch of the pain, the anger, the sorrow and the failure. Then she shoved it down.

She couldn't afford to wallow in it. There were always more patients, more injured, more people depending on her.

As she tugged her gloves off and scrubbed her hands, she relaxed the tiniest fraction. She loved her job, even when it sucked. Being a doctor...it was her calling. Before the invasion, she'd loved the high-pressure atmosphere of the ER, and had grand plans for her career. After a short time dabbling with surgery, she'd committed herself to emergency medicine. She'd loved the pressure, loved the idea of running her own ER one day.

Perhaps she should have been careful about what she wished for. Because now, she was in the ultimate high-pressure job and, for better or worse, she was the boss of medical.

Limited equipment, a motley mix of staff with varying backgrounds, and an unending stream of sick and injured.

She rubbed her now-clean hands against her face. She needed some coffee. Needed to get this nagging tiredness to take hike.

Sleep would be best, but that wasn't going to happen. She hadn't slept well for two weeks.

As she hit the tiny kitchenette in the corner of the infirmary to make her coffee, a lump lodged in her throat. She'd spent too any nights lately in a lather of sweat, fighting back screams.

Damn raptors.

She thought of the man who'd died on her table. He'd been the one who deserved nightmares about their alien aggressors, not Emerson. She'd been their prisoner for maybe an hour. Sure, they'd beaten her, but she'd survived.

Hell Squad had rescued her. And the team's toughest soldier, Gabe Jackson, had held her as she'd cried.

Emerson sipped her coffee. She didn't deserve to have flashbacks and be traumatized by what amounted to nothing by most of her patients' standards. The caffeine hit her bloodstream. Much better. Still, if she didn't get some sleep soon, she might need to consider a sedative.

Nope. Her entire body rebelled at the thought. Not an option. If she got called out of bed in the middle of the night—which happened on an awfully regular basis—she needed all her senses sharp, not fuzzy from drugs.

She spun, walking past the line of infirmary beds. Currently only one bed was occupied—by a teenager with a bad case of the flu. It was a minor miracle. She'd recently gotten all the raptor-experimentation patients cleared to live in their own quarters in the base. Most had to come back for regular monitoring and treatments. But, for their recovery, being in their own space was important.

"Doc!"

Emerson jolted, Norah's shout almost making her spill her coffee. "What?"

"Hell Squad's on their way in. One of them is injured."

Emerson's heart stopped. Squad Six, also known as Hell Squad, was one of the base's commando squads. Every day the squads—made up of any soldiers and officers from any and all branches of the military and police forces who'd survived the initial alien attacks—went out to do reconnaissance, rescue survivors, protect the base and fight the aliens.

Hell Squad was the roughest, toughest and deadliest of the squads.

They mowed through aliens like a laser scalpel.

"Who's injured?" she asked, setting her coffee down.

Norah bustled around to get Exam Room One ready. "The scary one. Gabe."

Emerson felt as though the floor had shifted beneath her. She pressed a palm to the wall. *He'd be fine.* Nothing could keep Gabe down for long.

The doors to the infirmary burst open and Emerson turned. Gabe was being carried between two other men—Marcus, Hell Squad's leader, and Cruz, the second-in-command. The muscular men had their arms around the bigger, taller Gabe. Thankfully, their black carbon-fiber armor had a built-in, light exoskeleton that helped with lifting, because at six and a half feet of tightly-packed muscle, she knew Gabe wasn't light.

She stared at his blood-splattered face, her stomach clenching. Turbulent gray eyes looked back at her. He was alive, conscious, and mostly on his feet—that was what was important.

"Over here." She pushed back the curtain and waved them in. Norah hovered nearby. Emerson gestured at the nurse with a jerk of her head. "Finish up, Norah. I can take care of this."

The woman raised her brows. "Okay. Not going to argue with you, Doc. Phillip is on duty tonight and in the office if you need help."

"Thanks." Phillip was a paramedic, and he, along with his boyfriend, Rick, were key parts of her medical team. Emerson yanked the curtain across.

"Not sitting on the fucking table," Gabe growled in a low voice.

"You'll do as ordered," Marcus growled back.

Hell Squad's leader had a voice that sounded like gravel and a scarred face that went with it.

"Chair," Gabe insisted.

Emerson pursed her lips. He was scratched up, deep gouges in his armor. *Through his armor.* She hissed in a breath. What the hell had gotten through his armor?

"Just put him in the chair," Emerson bustled forward. She didn't have time for them to have a pissing match. "Cruz, out."

The lean, handsome man stepped back far enough to be out of the way, and crossed his arms over his chest. "I'll stay. You might need help to hold him down. Or beat sense into his rock-hard head." His accent—American with a large dose of Mexican—had driven most of the base's single females into fits of delight, until he'd up and paired himself with a woman almost as dangerous as Hell Squad. The single ladies were still in mourning.

Emerson huffed out a breath. "Fine. Just stay back." She moved to Gabe and stepped between his legs. She pulled her portable m-scanner out of her lab coat. It was getting a little dented and was prone to shorting out at inconvenient times. Noah Kim, head of the tech team, had repaired it multiple times already, but he'd warned her it was on its last legs.

She ran the scanner over Gabe. "What happened, big guy?"

"Raptors."

She rolled her eyes. Gabe was a man of few words, but still. "I've never seen them tear through armor."

"Idiot went off half-cocked." Cruz's voice sizzled with anger. "Tore into them like Rambo."

"I was—"

"You should have waited for the team." Marcus did not sound happy.

The scanner beeped, and as she read the results, the tightness in her chest loosened. No major damage. Some minor blood loss, and some very deep gouges that had to hurt like hell. "You're lucky. You won't need surgery, just a small dose of nano-meds."

His impassive face didn't change, but she got the impression he wasn't happy about even getting nano-meds. The microscopic machines had revolutionized medicine fifty years back. A dose could heal a person in hours, instead of days or weeks. But they needed professional medical monitoring, or they could get out of control and wind up killing the patient.

She touched the jagged armor. "Let's get this off."

He sat still and silent as she leaned over his broad shoulders, stripping the armor off. She felt the heat pouring off his dark skin. Marcus held out a hand and took the armor from her. When she stepped back and finally got a good look at Gabe's injuries, she hissed. They appeared far worse than the scanner indicated. The left side of his chest was a bloody, ragged mess of scratches. In one, she swore she saw the flash of rib bones. "Gabe."

"It's fine."

She grabbed her pressure injector, dialed up a painkiller, and before he could protest, slammed it against the side of his thick neck.

Gray eyes bored into hers.

Cruz had a handsome face, but Emerson found Gabe's so much more compelling. She'd seen his medical report, so she knew his father had been African-American. His skin was a deep, dark bronze, and with his shaved head, strong features, and storm-gray eyes, he was worth a second or third look. But he also radiated a menacing, dangerous intensity that had most people searching for a hiding place.

Gabe didn't appear to notice or care. Apart from with his squad members, he didn't socialize.

And since he'd lost his twin brother to the raptors almost three months before, he'd withdrawn even more. That dangerous edge turning razor sharp.

She grabbed some up some sterile cleaning pads and set to work washing the blood away.

"He gonna live, Doc?" Marcus asked.

"Yes. The nano-meds will have this healed up in an hour or so."

"You got lucky, Gabe." Marcus shook his head. "You've held it together this long, don't lose it now."

Gabe remained stubbornly silent.

"The last two weeks, you've been taking more and more risks in the field."

Emerson's eyes widened. *What?* Since that mission to recover the patients, and her moment of captivity?

Marcus crossed his muscular arms. "You're going to get hurt worse than this, or get yourself killed."

Gabe's jaw worked. "I'll do what I have to do take down as many alien bastards as I can."

Marcus slammed a closed fist into the exam table, the metal rattling. Emerson jumped.

Marcus' face twisted. "If you don't care if you die, think of your fucking team, then. You'll get one of them killed if you keep this up." Hell Squad's leader turned and stormed out.

Cruz shot Gabe a sympathetic look. "Get your shit together. I've said it before, and I'll say it again. If you need to talk, I'm here." He nodded at Emerson and left.

Emerson prepared the nano-med injection, measuring out the correct dose. She hooked a monitor up to Gabe. "Is what they said true?"

"I don't want to kill myself."

His voice was toneless and her heart tripped in her chest. He might not want to commit suicide, but he didn't much care if he died, as long as he took out as many raptors as he could when he did.

"Zeke wouldn't want this—"

"I don't want to talk about him."

The fierce growl made her sigh. "Fine."

Gabe gripped her wrist. "I'm going to kill every single damn raptor in Sydney. That way the one who shot Zeke and the ones who fucking beat you black-and-blue will be dead."

She couldn't look away from him. They stared at each other, the silence stretching between them.

Then he released her. "Do it."

The thought of him taking reckless risks, getting himself killed, had her anger spiking. She jabbed the injector into his arm harder than she should have. He grunted.

She watched the metallic-silver liquid drain from the injector, the tiny machines powering into his blood stream.

His gaze never left hers. She saw the muscles in his neck strain and he gritted his teeth. His body tensed, his back arching slightly. The nano-meds hurt on the way in, and right now they were replicating fast, traveling through his bloodstream and targeting the areas that needed healing.

"You keep taking risks out in the field, you'll end up dead." She wanted to touch him, to smooth a hand down his stubbled cheek. She shoved her hands in her lab coat instead.

"Don't need a lecture," he rasped between clenched teeth.

No, he wanted very little from her. She'd learned that the hard way. "Zeke wouldn't want this." She raised her voice. "Phillip?"

"Yes, Doc?" The tall man appeared, peering around the curtain.

Emerson shoved the electronic tablet at him. "Please monitor Mr. Jackson's nano-med infusion. Don't let him leave until you say he can."

Phillip cast a dubious look at Gabe, as if

weighing up their differences in height and weight. "Okay."

"I'm off to grab something to eat." And shower the day's hardships away. She cast a final glance at Gabe.

He was staring at the floor.

If he wanted to kill himself, there was nothing she could do about it. Her heart hurting a little, Emerson strode out of the infirmary.

READY FOR ANOTHER?

ACTION
ADVENTURE
TREASURE HUNTS
SEXY SCI-FI ROMANCE

Dr. Eos Rai has spent a lifetime dedicated to her mother's dream of finding the long-lost *Mona Lisa*. When Eos uncovers tantalizing evidence of Star's End—the last known location of the masterpiece—she's shocked when her employer, the Galactic Institute of Historic Preservation, refuses to back her expedition. Left with no choice, Eos must trust the most notorious treasure hunter in the galaxy, a man she finds infuriating, annoying and far too tempting.

Dathan Phoenix can sniff out relics at a stellar mile. With his brothers by his side, he takes the adventures that suit him and refuses to become a lazy, bitter failure like their father. When the gorgeous Eos Rai comes looking to hire him, he knows she's trouble, but he's lured into a hunt that turns into a wild and dangerous adventure. As Eos and Dathan are pushed to their limits, they discover treasure isn't the only thing they're drawn to...but how will their desire survive when Dathan demands the *Mona Lisa* as his payment?

The Phoenix Adventures

At Star's End
In the Devil's Nebula
On a Rogue Planet
Beneath a Trojan Moon
Beyond Galaxy's Edge
On a Cyborg Planet

Also by Anna Hackett

Hell Squad
Marcus
Cruz
Gabe
Reed

The Anomaly Series
Time Thief
Mind Raider
Soul Stealer
Salvation

Perma Series
Winter Fusion

The WindKeepers Series
Wind Kissed, Fire Bound
Taken by the South Wind
Tempting the West Wind
Defying the North Wind
Claiming the East Wind

Standalone Titles
Savage Dragon
Hunter's Surrender
One Night with the Wolf

Anthologies
A Galactic Holiday
Moonlight (UK only)
Vampire Hunter (UK only)
Awakening the Dragon (UK Only)

About the Author

I'm passionate about **_action romance_**. I love stories that combine the thrill of falling in love with the excitement of action, danger and adventure. I'm a sucker for that moment when the team is walking in slow motion, shoulder-to-shoulder heading off into battle. I write about people overcoming unbeatable odds and achieving seemingly impossible goals. I like to believe it's possible for all of us to do the same.

My books are mixture of action, adventure and sexy romance and they're recommended for anyone who enjoys fast-paced stories where the boy wins the girl at the end (or sometimes the girl wins the boy!)

For release dates, action romance info, free books, and other fun stuff, sign up for the latest news here:

Website: AnnaHackettBooks.com

Printed in Great Britain
by Amazon

36185850R00139